D0671265

THAT JULIA REDFERN

Julia Redfern—and trouble—seem to go hand in hand. Julia tries to be good, but crazy things just happen to her. Riding her brother Greg's bike straight down the hill— and nearly into large bossy Aunt Alex—was one. So was giving her big, flossy doll Felony to the grinling, the creature who lived in the garden. But some strange and wonderful things happen to Julia, too. Things that have to do with her father's dream of becoming a writer—and with the people she loves the most.

"Cameron conveys Julia's rich personality in a wonderfully readable way; and young readers will love meeting her. . . ."

—*School Library Journal* (Starred review)

PUFFIN BOOKS BY ELEANOR CAMERON

Julia's Magic
That Julia Redfern
Julia and the Hand of God
A Room Made of Windows
The Private Worlds of Julia Redfern

That
Julia Redfern

by Eleanor Cameron

illustrated by Gail Owens

AVONDALE MIDDLE SCHOOL MEDIA CENTER
1445 W. Auburn Road
Rochester Hills, MI 48309-4159

PUFFIN BOOKS

PUFFIN BOOKS

Published by the Penguin Group

Viking Penguin, a division of Penguin Books USA Inc.,
40 West 23rd Street, New York, New York 10010, U.S.A.
Penguin Books Ltd, 27 Wrights Lane, London W8 5TZ, England
Penguin Books Australia Ltd, Ringwood, Victoria, Australia
Penguin Books Canada Ltd, 2801 John Street, Markham, Ontario, Canada L3R 1B4
Penguin Books (N.Z.) Ltd, 182–90 Wairau Road, Auckland 10, New Zealand

Penguin Books Ltd, Registered Offices: Harmondsworth, Middlesex, England

First published in the United States of America by E. P. Dutton,
a division of Penguin Books USA Inc., 1982
Published in Puffin Books 1989

1 3 5 7 9 10 8 6 4 2

Text copyright © Eleanor Cameron, 1982
Illustrations copyright © E. P. Dutton, a division of Penguin Books USA Inc., 1982
All rights reserved

LIBRARY OF CONGRESS CATALOGING-IN-PUBLICATION DATA
Cameron, Eleanor, 1912–
That Julia Redfern / by Eleanor Cameron ; illustrated by Gail Owens.   p.   cm.
Sequel: Julia and the hand of God.
Sequel to: Julia's magic.
Summary: Family loss and other unexpected, even strange occurrences
cannot dampen for long the spirits of the irrepressible Julia.
ISBN 0-14-034041-6
[1. Family life—Fiction.]   I. Owens, Gail, ill.   II. Title.
[PZ7.C143Th 1989]   [Fic]—dc19   89-30229

Printed in the United States of America
by R. R. Donnelley & Sons Company, Harrisonburg, Virginia
Set in Garamond #3

Except in the United States of America, this book is sold subject to the
condition that it shall not, by way of trade or otherwise, be lent,
re-sold, hired out, or otherwise circulated without the publisher's prior
consent in any form of binding or cover other than that in which it is
published and without a similar condition including this condition being
imposed on the subsequent purchaser.

11/94 perma $8.35

This book is for
Elizabeth Venturelli

Contents

1

Greg's Bike

The heat was enough to make anyone dizzy, this fierce golden light pouring down into the berry garden. Julia went weaving along the narrow path through the vines, got as far as the side gate, and there was Greg's bike leaning against the gatepost.

She stared at it with her usual huge desire and longing. What she loved best in the world were Mama and Daddy and Uncle Hugh and Patchy-cat and Sister—and Greg's bike. But she wasn't to be allowed one until later. Mama said she'd be too much of a danger, an absolute menace, on a bike of her own.

Greg was always supposed to put his away in the garage at the back of the house, but this time he'd forgotten. He'd had something more important to do, and Julia knew what it was. She jogged over to the fence and peered through, and there, sure enough, were Greg and Bob, his faithful bosom friend, down on their knees in Bob's backyard sorting over their old streetcar junk.

Julia turned and studied Greg's bike again. She'd pictured herself times without number whizzing down hills, jumping the bike over a curb into the street and leaping it up onto the sidewalk on the other side, just as easy as anything, the way Greg always did. Then flashing around the playground at school and past Maisie's house, with Maisie out in front watching, her eyes big, and Julia airily waving and disappearing on down the street, leaving Maisie behind looking after her.

"Julia," said her father, coming out of the vines with a big blue bowl full of blackberries, "Aunt Alex and Uncle Hugh are going to drop by, so come on in now and get cleaned up. You look rather purplish as to mouth and paws." And he went off along the path and up the steps and into the house singing in a deep, rich voice,

> Tell me, tell me,
> Where do flies go
> In - the - win-ter - time?
> Do they go to gay Par-eeee?

Julia frowned, furiously working things out. Then she went over to the bike, led it tenderly along to the sidewalk, and up the street to the top of the gentle slope that ended at the corner behind her house. And her heart was beating so hard with excitement and fright that she could feel her chest shaking.

At the top of the hill she turned and looked back down. And there, on the other side of the street, was a little wiry, flying figure, arms waving, pigtails leaping out behind.

"You're gonna get it!" shrieked Maisie. "You're gonna get it—you just wait. Are you ever gonna get it! *Greg's bike!*"

Julia let the bike crash and took off after Maisie. "You mind your own business," she yelled. "You shut up and mind your own—" but Maisie had already turned and whisked off home again, bounced up her front steps, was in at the front door, and had banged it behind her before Julia could so much as get to Maisie's front walk. She stood there panting with wrath—what if Greg had heard? Then she turned and ran up to the top of the hill again. Nothing could stop her now, *nothing,* except if Greg should come scrabbling over the fence and out into the street after her. But he was nowhere in sight.

She got the bike up again and tilted it so that she could fling a leg over and hoist her behind onto the seat. Then she gave a push to get it upright. It wobbled. Wildly her feet searched for the pedals, but couldn't reach. And before the bike wavered sideways again, the slope took hold of them and away they went, slowly just for a second or two, then with horrible speed.

Julia was leaning forward, fingers desperately gripping the handlebars, eyes staring, mouth ajar, though no cry came, legs spraddled stiff. The long slope pulled them as if it were a hand, faster—faster—faster, and the pulling kept them steady.

A car had drawn alongside the curb and Uncle Hugh had gotten out, then come around to help Aunt Alex. He was standing with his back to Julia as Aunt Alex walked past him to the sidewalk and looked up the hill. Her mouth opened but, as with Julia, no cry would come. She pointed, waved her hands in terror —Julia was headed straight for them.

Uncle Hugh turned. And just as Julia was about to smash into them, he jerked Aunt Alex back at the very last second. Julia zinged past, the bicycle scraped the telephone pole, and she was hurled through the air and landed on the pavement on her back like a bug with her legs up. "Oh!" she gasped. "Oh! O-o-oh!" She was too stunned to cry. *Greg's ruined bike—his ruined, mashed-up bike! What would he say? What would he do to her?*

"That wicked child—oh, that wicked, *wicked* child! Hugh, she could have killed me. She could have injured me for life. And Greg's bicycle—!"

Julia opened her eyes and gazed up at them. She made out the very large shape of Aunt Alex, a big white blur, and the dark, much slimmer shape of Uncle Hugh. Aunt Alex was standing, her hands pressed to her broad bosom, and there was a white hat like a platter set at a slant on her head. Uncle Hugh was kneeling beside Julia, but now he and Aunt Alex floated strangely away, came back, and floated off again.

"Uncle Hugh, I didn't mean—I didn't know—!"

"No," stormed Aunt Alex. "Of course not, Julia Redfern. You never do mean or know. Get up now." Uncle Hugh helped her and she put her arms around his neck and gave him a hug. And he gave her one back with a kiss on the cheek.

"Are you all in one piece?"

When they had determined that no bones were broken, Uncle Hugh righted Greg's bike and gave it a thorough going-over.

"Scraped and bent!" exclaimed Aunt Alex with passion. "Buckled beyond repair, I haven't a doubt. And new only last Christmas."

"Not at all, Alex," said Uncle Hugh. "It's perfectly all right," and he wheeled it over to the fence and set it against the gatepost, just as Greg had left it. "Come now, Julia," he said, holding out his hand, "let's go in and not make a fuss—no harm done."

"But Celia and Harry should certainly be told," declared Aunt Alex, moving majestically ahead and carefully stepping over a break in the front walk that

Daddy should have fixed months ago, "that Julia almost killed me. There is no reason on earth why that child's parents—"

"Yes, yes, I know, Alex. I know. But we've come for a visit, to have a little pleasure—"

And so, after Aunt Alex had been indignant all the way along the walk, they went up onto the porch and inside. Julia tiptoed quickly away down the hall to her own room while the hellos and how-are-you's and just-fine's were being said. She hovered for a moment or two at her bedroom door, inside the room with just her head peeking out. And she heard Daddy go into the kitchen, saying he was going to give them all fresh blackberries and cream and hot buttered muffins.

"Celia," said Aunt Alex to Mama, who got home from work at the music store early on Saturdays, "I think you should be told, without my making a scene, that I have just—"

"Oh, now, Alex!" said Uncle Hugh.

"—that I have just been almost run into and most horribly injured, and Greg's new bicycle almost demolished. Would you believe it, Julia took off from the top of the hill—the *top* of the hill, mind you, at her age—and came straight for me—"

"On Greg's bike?"

"On Greg's bike," pronounced Aunt Alex deeply, like a Fate. "And it is my firm opinion, Celia, that that child—"

Abruptly, Julia closed the door and sat down on her bed. She swallowed, and her heart began to beat the way it had when she was taking the bike out onto the sidewalk, knowing exactly what she was going to do and that she was determined to do it. Then, hearing footsteps, she got up and was about to slip hastily out the french doors that led into the garden when the hall door opened and there was Mama. She stood and looked at Julia. Julia looked at her.

Silence.

Then Mama came over and gave her a short, sharp spanking. "You have been a very, very naughty girl. Aunt Alex is right. You could have injured her terribly —and Uncle Hugh, too."

"Does Daddy—?" But the tears were bulging over and she couldn't finish.

"Of course he knows. Now get cleaned up and come out and sit quietly." And Mama closed the door and went away.

2

—⬥⬥⬥—

Pull Down
the Blinds

When Julia came into the living room, having put on a clean dress and given her face a swipe with a wet facecloth, nobody paid her the least attention. Uncle Hugh was talking to Daddy in the kitchen and Aunt Alex and Mama were coming out of the bedroom. They were going on about clothes.

But now, to Julia's horror, Aunt Alex was headed straight for Sister's chair. It was a small one, heavy, upholstered, with arms like a big chair, and surely it would not hold Aunt Alex, who had never thought to try and sit in it before.

She turned and was beginning to lower herself when "*No,* Aunt Alex," burst out Julia, and Aunt Alex started and straightened as if she'd been hit with a stick. "That's Sister's chair. She's there—you're going to sit on her—"

"Oh, don't be *ridic*ulous, Julia!" Aunt Alex's face, under her big white hat, had gotten all red. "You know perfectly well you've made up Sister. There is no such person—you just imagine her," and she plopped right down on top of Sister, filling the little chair completely.

Julia, shocked, and with a strange hollow feeling in her stomach, sat down opposite and studied Aunt Alex. Sister had disappeared. But where had she gone? Had she slipped out from under just before Aunt Alex's bottom hit the chair? Julia couldn't see her anywhere.

Now Uncle Hugh and her father came in with plates with the berry bowls on them and the hot muffins, just like for Flopsy, Mopsy, and Cotton-tail in the story.

"Haven't you already had a lot of berries this morning, Julia?" Daddy asked when he gave her hers.

"Not very many. Just a few."

"Oh, but I'm disappointed Greg isn't here!" cried Aunt Alex. "Where's my Greg? Hugh, go outside and call. Maybe he's only next door. And when you go out, get my sweater out of the car. It's folded up in my bag with the war knitting. My, but you keep your house cold, Celia. It's always much sunnier over here in Berkeley than it is in San Francisco, but I just freeze in this shadowy little house."

"That's funny," said Julia. "Daddy says big people

don't feel things like that like little skinny ones do."

"Julia," said Daddy rather loudly, "skip on out and call Greg and get Aunt Alex's sweater."

"No, no," said Aunt Alex. "Hugh knows right where it is."

So off went Uncle Hugh, leaving his muffin to get cold, and Mama went into Greg's room and came back with a sheet of paper.

"Alex," she said, "I thought you'd like to see what Greg's been up to. He showed us this, part of a story, so I don't think he'd mind you seeing—"

"Oh, I can read it—I can read it!" shouted Julia. "Let me, Mama—"

"Now, Julia," said Aunt Alex, glancing over the paper, "I'm quite sure you couldn't read this. Your little fairy stories and the Beatrix Potter books, perhaps, but not this."

"But I *can!* Please let me show you. Please?" And so Aunt Alex handed over the paper and Julia began, even though she couldn't seem to understand what it was all about.

" 'But until we get this straightened out,' " she read slowly, " 'I'm going to take the whole lot of you down to the police station and hold you on suspicion of contempt, telling fairy stories, and just common ordinary lying to the lawfully elected sheriff of this county. And I shall hold you there pending trial before a suitable court on the charge of burglary in the first, second, and third degrees, with com-pli-ca-tions as here-in-before stated, on information supplied by C. Jimson Camphor, here-in-after to be known as the party of the first part, his hires and as—' Well, I don't know that word—'forever.' "

Julia looked up in triumph, and Aunt Alex was staring at her.

"I can't believe it," she breathed presently. "I simply cannot believe it."

"See, Aunt Alex, see? I *told* you—"

"But of course the boy's a genius," announced Aunt Alex, shaking her head and waving her hand as if Greg were too much for her, "to be able to write a thing like that at the age of eight. As if he were twenty!"

"But I read it!" shouted Julia, hot with indignation. "You said I couldn't, but I *did!*"

Aunt Alex held up a hand. "That will do, Julia. No need to raise your voice—I can hear. As I was saying, Greg absolutely amazes me. That boy is positively brilliant, and later on, when he begins to—"

But Julia heard no more. Just as Uncle Hugh came back with Aunt Alex's sweater, and with the news that Greg was nowhere within calling distance, she felt a stinging rising in her throat. And there was that awful burning in the place under her tongue that meant she'd better make off for the bathroom as fast as she could.

She leaned over the toilet and up surged everything.

Blackberries, cream, hot buttered muffin, and all those berries she'd had before the ones in the bowl, eaten in the garden.

"Oh, Julia," said Mama, coming in, "and you told us you hadn't had any this morning."

Julia couldn't answer at once. Then, rather muffled and exhausted, "Well, I said not many—"

"All the same," and Mama took her to the washbasin and wiped off her hot face, "it might not be just that. Sometimes Aunt Alex doesn't seem to understand, does she? Come, now, off with your shoes and dress and into bed with you—"

"Into *bed!* But I haven't talked to Uncle Hugh—"

"Later—when you've calmed down."

Julia lay on her side, curled into a ball, and Mama went over and pulled down the blinds on the french doors.

"You've forgotten something," said Julia. "The camomile tea. Remember? Mrs. Rabbit gave a dose of it to Peter—one tablespoon at bedtime after he'd eaten all those beans and radishes."

"What a pity I don't have any." Mama leaned over and gave Julia a kiss. "We should do everything just right, shouldn't we?"

Julia clung to her, and after Mama had gone out and closed the door, Julia looked for Sister. Maybe they could tell Continued Stories. Maybe she could go on with the story she'd been telling Patchy-cat and Sister

out in the garden when Daddy had been picking berries—the one about the big fat bossy queen and the
nice kind handsome king. But strangely, Sister wasn't
there. She had disappeared completely, for the first
time Julia could ever remember, after Aunt Alex had
sat down in the little armchair. Never before had Sister
failed to be in this room when Julia was here. But by
the time Julia had fallen asleep, she still hadn't come.

3

Much, Much
Too Big

And she never did come back. She was gone for good.

Julia pretended she was there. She tried making up that Sister was sitting at the end of the bed when they told each other Continued Stories before Julia went to sleep at night or early in the morning before anybody else was up. But it was no use. And Julia would think about Sister very sharply at times when she wasn't playing or quarreling with Maisie, or reading a book from the library. And when she was telling one of her stories to the Japanese dolls and Patchy out in the garden, she thought of her especially, because there was no Sister to sit and listen with the rest.

"Julia," said Mama one morning when they were

having breakfast a few days before Daddy had to leave for the army camp where he was going to fly a plane, "it seems to me you haven't said anything about Sister lately. Has she gone away?"

"I don't know. She disappeared when Aunt Alex sat down on her in Sister's special chair. I warned Aunt Alex, but she said I was silly. She said don't be ridiculous. And Sister hasn't come back."

"Thank *good*ness!" shouted Greg, buttering his fourth slice of toast with great slabs of butter.

"That's quite enough, Greg," said Daddy. "Scrape some of it off—it's enough to make anyone queasy just to watch you."

"What's queasy?" asked Julia. That was a good word, one she'd never heard before. She liked the sound—quee-ee-eezy.

"Sickish—the way you felt when you hustled off to the bathroom after all those blackberries you ate the other day."

"Oh, for the love of Mike," said Greg in disgust. "What's this mean, what's that mean, what does everything mean? A person can't say a single word—"

"That's all right," said Daddy. "If she's going to be a writer—"

"*Is* she, Harry!" Mama looked at him with an expression that was both solemn and surprised. "You've never said that before."

"No, but I've thought it—off and on. And if she's

going to be a writer, she has to know about words, and she might as well begin early. She has to keep on asking and finding out. But it seems to come naturally."

"Who says Julia's going to be a writer?" demanded Greg. "How can anyone tell when she's so young?"

"I can tell," said Daddy quietly. "I can tell. I prophesy."

"What's prof—?" began Julia, then stopped and made another ditch in her porridge for the milk to run out to the river. Then she scooped the bed of the river deeper so that the milk could run to the sea, which was over on the other side of the bowl.

"It means," said Daddy, "to see and to know and to tell ahead of time. Of course she'll be a writer."

"But what about Greg?" asked Mama. "What's he going to be? I thought for sure it would be Greg who would—"

"Oh, a certain kind, maybe, a science writer or a news reporter. He could be anything. I can't tell. But he's no good at making up. Julia will write stories, the way I— Oh, Lord, no!" And Daddy closed his eyes for a second and struck his hand to his forehead so that a piece of dark hair flopped down over it. "I hope *not* the way I do!"

There was a little silence among them because he could write only Saturdays and Sundays after being at work all week, and his stories in their large, tan envelopes usually came back from whatever magazine he sent them to. And this could turn him into someone who didn't talk or smile and who went off by himself —someone completely different from the person he was most of the time.

"Anyway," said Greg, "most little kids are good at making up stories."

"Yes," said Daddy. "So they are. But you can argue with me all you like—I know what I know." And he got up and said he was going out to the garage to get on with his project, which he wanted to finish before he went away.

Nobody knew a thing about this project. "I hope your mother will like it," was all he'd say, and so everybody thought it must be for her, a going-away present, only the other way around. Not a present for the one who was leaving, but for the one who was left.

"Anything you make, I bet I'll like," Mama said. "But what on earth can it be?"

Julia and Mama went shopping that afternoon at Hinks on Shattuck Avenue to get Daddy some things he would need to take with him. And when they got home with their packages, he was just coming out of the bathroom in his bathrobe and scrubbing away at his wet thick hair as if he'd been cleaning up for the going-away party tonight at Aunt Alex and Uncle Hugh's.

"I've finished," he said. "Finished my project, and now you can come and look and see what you think of it."

Well, there was nothing new in the living room, and Daddy didn't turn to cross it toward Greg's or his and Mama's bedroom. He turned to the left along the little hall that led to Julia's room. She couldn't believe it. And when they got to her door, he stood to one side and motioned them in, and there—near the french doors, just beyond her chest of drawers and across from the little empty space at the end of her bed—was a sort of table.

It *was* a table, only not a plain, ordinary one such as you would put a cloth on and plates and knives and forks. Nor a book laid at an angle with a potted plant and an ornament or two. This was a special table because it had a wide drawer in the middle, wide but not very deep, and two deeper drawers, one on each side.

Julia stared at it, and her mother and father never said a word while she turned the sight of that table over in her mind. Of course—it was a desk.

Her father had put bookends on it to hold her books, and these were standing along the back of it against the wall. There was a lamp on it, and a blotter, and a tall sort of cup, but with no handle, to hold pencils—and there were sharpened pencils in it. And her one chair was drawn up in front of the desk, all ready for her to sit down and read, or write something.

Julia went slowly over to it and put her hand out and ran it over the surface. It was just as smooth as could be, wonderfully smooth, with a faint gloss, and it was honey-colored. Well, a little deeper, as dark as dark honey. Honey brown. Now Julia drew out her chair and sat down, and noticed how the leaf-patterned sunlight at this time of day slanted in across the length of her desk, across her right shoulder. She opened the middle drawer—how quietly it came out—and then the other two. They fitted so beautifully that if you gave them the slightest push, they slid right in.

All at once Julia put her head down on the desk, facing her parents, and stretched her arms across it as if to enfold it.

"Do you like it, Julia?" asked Daddy. But he could tell, and his face had lighted up.

She was silent for an instant. "It's my best present, ever," she said finally, solemnly, in a low voice. "My very best present."

"And look," he said, coming over, "I didn't put any knobs on the bottoms of the legs so that when you need it to be higher, someone can put them on. And we must get you a firm pillow for your chair to raise you up for now."

"What do you mean," demanded Mama, her eyes widening, and she spoke too loudly as if she were angry, "*someone* can put them on?"

"Oh, well—I didn't mean anything. It's only that no

one can possibly know how long this confounded war will last—"

And then, "Mrrah-mrrah?" said Patchy-cat, pushing one of the french doors open with his head just enough to let himself in and announcing his presence the way he always did. He was a big, glossy cat, mostly black, with one white ear, a white chest, a splash of white on his back, and a white tip to his tail, which was always moving as though it had a language of its own. He took one look at Julia's desk and went right to it, as if he recognized it as his territory. He hopped up, bunched himself in a nice, warm piece of sunlight, and settled down with his front paws tucked under and his tail curled neatly round.

Now there was a movement at the french doors and there stood Greg and Gramma, looking in, staring at the desk. Gramma came in first. She had a package that she tossed on Julia's bed, the things she'd been knitting for Daddy to take away to camp with him. And she never took her eyes from the desk.

"Golly Moses," said Greg. "So it was for Julia." And Julia knew, just the way he said it, that that desk was exactly what *he* would have wanted.

Gramma drew in her breath. "But it's too big!" she exclaimed. "It's much, much too big for the size of this room, Harry. And it's ridiculous for a child Julia's age. It should be for Greg—"

"I don't see why for Greg," said Daddy, smiling his

odd little folded-in smile that he always met Gramma's irritations with. "Greg will have my desk and type-writer while I'm gone—why should I make him some-thing he doesn't need? And besides, I built a bookcase for him. Remember?"

"Well, it's too big," she persisted. "Why didn't you make her a *little* desk if you think she has to have one? But imagine, a child with a desk like that—! You know, Harry, the whole trouble with you is, you just spoil that child. You're fatuous."

"What's that?" said Julia. "What's fatch—?

Mama laughed. "Addled in the head about some-one, too fond, finding no fault."

"What's addled?" said Julia.

4

Felony

"Hello, everybody—hello, hello!" sang out Uncle Dick at the party that night for Daddy. He was a stout, tall, cheery man whose habit it was to lift Julia and swing her up and tell her she was getting so big he could hardly lift her. But he always did, every time just the same. Aunt Mim, very small compared to her husband, gave her a good hug because they didn't see each other very often, and then here came Aunt Alex and that delicious smell of the perfume she always wore.

"A surprise for you, Julia," she said. "Remember we didn't have your birthday present for you in time? Well, it finally arrived."

"Good grief," said Julia. "*Another* surprise—two in one day!"

Everybody looked at her.

"What was the first one?" asked Aunt Mim.

"Oh, boy, you should just see it!" shouted Greg. "Dad made it. It's a desk four feet long and two and a half feet wide and two and a half feet high, and it's got three drawers, a wide one in the middle and thicker ones on the sides and it's perfectly huge and it'll hardly go in her room."

"So now you're ready to begin your life, Julia," said Uncle Hugh, smiling at her as if he'd already known what her father was up to. "Really begin it."

"But, Harry," said Aunt Alex, "why such a big one? Why not a nice little one? It sounds as if it should be for Greg. After all, *he's* going to be the writer. Which reminds me, you did finish your story, Greg? I've been telling Uncle Dick and Aunt Miriam all about C. Jimson Camphor and they can't wait to—"

"But, Aunt Alex, I said there was just that little bit. And there isn't any more, and there never will be any more. And I'm not going to *be* a writer—I'm going to be a streetcar inspector."

Aunt Alex studied him, and Uncle Hugh chuckled and winked at Uncle Dick and Aunt Mim. "I don't want to hear anything about streetcar inspectors," said Aunt Alex. "I'm not in the least interested in streetcar inspectors. Hugh, do you want to get—?" And when

Uncle Hugh had come back with a large box wrapped in pink paper and tied up with a fluffy pink bow, Aunt Alex gave it to Julia. "This is more what I would have liked as a child."

Well, big as it is, thought Julia, you couldn't possibly get even a small bike into *this* box. She pulled off the paper and ribbon and lifted off the lid. And there was a doll, an absolutely enormous doll, white teeth glistening between curved lips, blue eyes shining glassily under thick lashes, glossy blonde hair tumbling around the fat bright cheeks, and dainty fingers all spread and curled in the most ladylike fashion.

After a little, "Well, what are you going to say, Julia?" prompted Mama anxiously. "I've never seen anything—I mean, that *size*—"

"The child's stunned," said Aunt Mim. "And I shouldn't wonder."

"Julia?" urged Mama.

"Thank you, Aunt Alex and Uncle Hugh," said Julia faintly. She looked up at Uncle Hugh and couldn't begin to imagine what he was thinking. He had the strangest expression. "Thank you," she said again, not knowing what she was saying. "Thank you."

"I knew you'd be overcome," cried Aunt Alex in triumph. "I knew it! Have you ever seen anything like her—almost as big as you are? And you know what, Julia? I didn't even think about Sister at the time I spoke up for her—she was in a Singer Sewing Machine window being used as a display. But when you lost Sister, I thought, why, it's like a miracle. Here's your new Sister, right here, to take the other Sister's place."

Julia gazed at Aunt Alex in shocked bewilderment. "But how did you know about—?"

"Why, your mother told Uncle Hugh, and he told me—that she doesn't seem to come around anymore. Isn't it perfect how it's all worked out?"

Julia couldn't answer. Her mind went to the time she'd told her king and queen story to the Japanese dolls and Patchy and Sister out in the garden, and all at once she felt terribly, terribly sad.

"What are you going to call her?" asked Aunt Mim gravely. "Your fine new doll."

"Felony," said Julia, without thinking or caring. "Felony Franklinburg."

"Felony!" Uncle Dick whistled. "Now, *there's* a name!" And he and Aunt Mim and Aunt Alex burst out laughing, and Julia looked at them and saw their mouths, the black pockets of laughter. But what was so funny about Felony for a name? "You see, Julia," said Uncle Dick, "it means a crime, like burglary or murder."

"Doesn't matter," said Julia. "Burglars and murdery. That's her name." And she hauled Felony out of the box and banged her down on a chair. "*Now,*" she whispered, "you *stay* there, and don't move or I'll wallop you," and went off to the kitchen to tell Hulda,

Aunt Alex's cook, all about this great big thing that was supposed to take Sister's place, and to hug Jennie, who was Uncle Hugh's collie.

When Hulda came in to clear away the dishes of the main course, Julia wanted to help, but Aunt Alex said the plates were far too valuable. However, Greg was allowed to help Hulda bring in the dessert, which was his and Julia's favorite—sweet, crusty, thin shells stuffed with ice cream and heaped up all over with strawberries and a big dollop of whipped cream on top. And if you got off your chair and got down on a level with the table and scraped the strawberries and whipped cream to one side, you could look into the shell as if it was a little house, and see a light shining through onto the ice cream. Kind of like a secret world, Julia thought. But Mama leaned over and whispered that she was to get back onto her chair at *once* and sit still and be a good, decent child.

However, Fate was against her, as it so often seemed to be.

There they all were, sitting finishing their desserts, Julia, like a good, decent child, arranging melted pink designs on her plate and the grown-ups chattering, when Aunt Mim let out a high, sharp cry.

"A mouse, Hugh! Oh, a mouse—over behind the curtain. I *saw* it—"

Instantly, everybody got up, and Uncle Dick

plunged out into the kitchen and came back with a broom. And Julia saw the mouse run out from behind the curtain and dart across under the dining table, making for the hall. And Uncle Dick came down hard with his broom when it got out from under the table, but missed.

"Run, Mrs. Tittlemouse, *run, run!*" shrieked Julia, racing into the hall ahead of Uncle Dick and seeing Mrs. Tittlemouse flatten her belly to the floor and run for her life. She was nothing but a little gray streak.

She got onto the Persian rug, with Uncle Dick whanging down with his broom and Julia clutching his arm and trying desperately to stop him. Mrs. Tittlemouse escaped just by the tip of her tail and got under a big chest of drawers. But when Uncle Dick scrabbled under it with the broom, she whipped out the far side. And Julia had by that time got to the front door ahead of her and snatched it open.

"*No,* Julia," shouted Aunt Alex, "shut that door instantly!"

But Julia held it wide, dancing and dancing with unbearable excitement and suspense. "*Run,* Mrs. Tittlemouse—" and out went Mrs. Tittlemouse into darkness and safety—no one knew where.

Julia felt what was coming. Quietly and solemnly she closed the front door and turned and faced everyone. Yes—Aunt Alex was furious.

"Julia Redfern," she said, her big dark eyes darting

sparks, "that mouse will now come right back in again. How *could* you let it out when I distinctly told you not to! Really, Celia—" and she turned to Mama as if words failed her.

"Oh, Julia," said Mama, "what *are* we to do with you!"

And all at once Julia had the most splendiferous idea. "Aunt Alex, *I* know—I don't deserve Felony! I've got to give her back to you. I've been very, very bad, and so you've got to take her back, haven't you! I absolutely *can't have her,* can I?"

But it didn't work.

Aunt Alex stared at Julia in astonishment. Then she gave a deep sort of exhausted sigh. "No, Julia—that's *not* the way. What you've got to do is behave yourself so that you *do* deserve that beautiful doll, as I'm sure, deep down in your heart, you really want to."

Blast and thunderation!

And she was banished to Uncle Hugh's study, where she lay kicking her heels in the air on his couch and seeing in her mind, just as clear as clear could be, Mrs. Tittlemouse sleaking her way under the grasses and bushes to where there was a tiny round hole in the side of the house into which Julia saw her vanish and knew she was going to her babies, asleep in the nest she had made.

5

___

Leaving

Run, run, Mrs. Tittlemouse *(sang Julia)*
Why did you go out of your little house
Into that great big one?
And Uncle Dick wanted to bash you
    with a broom
But I saved you—
Run, run, run, Mrs. Tittlemouse!

She turned over in bed and there was Felony sitting against one of the front legs of the desk in the moonlight, her back to the french door. Moonlight was gleaming across the floor, reflecting up onto Felony's face. The front of her was in shadow, but her glass eyes caught a hint of the light as though Felony were alive. *No, no!*

Julia flopped back so as not to have to look at her. But all at once she got up and went over and shoved her away under the desk so that Felony was hidden. She stood there looking out into the garden, into the maze of deep shadows and brilliant patches of silver the moon was sending down. Never had she seen the moonlight so bright. She was hardly ever awake in the middle of the night, and all at once she wanted to go out there and let that cool silvery light pour over her.

But of course she couldn't because of the grinling. She could never go out alone into the dark garden with the grinling hiding and waiting.

She hadn't any idea what it looked like because she had never seen it. It was too black, and it always hid in the shadows. But she knew it was there. The peculiar thing was that Julia never felt it was in the house, but that it always stayed in the garden and never came out in the daytime.

Patchy-cat knew about the grinling. Sometimes, out in the garden, when he had his hind leg stuck up in the air, holding it steady with one curled front paw and scrubbing away at it with his rough little tongue, he'd stop and stare and stare without blinking right at one spot way back under the bushes.

He was staring at the grinling. And it was Julia's private, awful, scarey secret. She'd never even told Uncle Hugh. But she knew what she'd do. She would

write a letter to Daddy to take with him, and she would
tell him her secret.

July 8

Dear Father   This is for you to read on the trane.
I am going to tell you about the grinling. Did you
know it is in the garden? It is out at night so I dont go
out there at night. If Mama wants me to I say I have
to go to the bathroom and then Greg can go out. Did
you ever see the grinling wen you and Mama were
out there at night? Patchy-cat knows it is there.
Somtimes when he is sleping and wakes up, he looks at
the grinling. His eers are moving and moving, and he
looks at one place. Maybe the grinling is saying
somthing. Please write and tell me if you know it
is there.

Love Julia

She folded her letter up very small and put it in her
desk drawer to give Daddy when he went away. And
it was all very strange, those last three days before he
left. Because all three mornings, right after breakfast,
he shut himself in the bedroom where his desk was.
And they heard his typewriter going *lickety-cut*—and
then long silences, then more banging away. And
Mama didn't mention a word about all he'd promised
to do before he left—fixing that crack in the front
walk, and the leaks in the roof, and the faucets that
dripped in the kitchen. Instead she took his lunch in to

him each noon so that he wouldn't have to come out and forget what he'd been thinking.

"Now, don't you say one word to anybody, Julia," Mama made her promise, "especially to Maisie Woollard, or she'll go right back and tell her mother and father. Mr. Woollard is so blasted handy around the house, I can hardly stand it. He fixes *everything*. I've never *known* such a man for fixing things. Never sits down for a second. As for Gramma, of course she'll have her two cents' worth about that walk."

And Gramma did, when she came over to say good-bye to Daddy, but it didn't matter, because Greg said *he'd* fix the walk. And over at the station in Oakland when Daddy was about to leave, Aunt Alex said she'd bet anything Greg could fix it as good as anybody, and then she wanted to know what Daddy had been doing these last three days. But he didn't say a word about staying in the bedroom typing the whole time, and neither did Mama.

Then here came the train, and Daddy kissed them all goodbye (except Uncle Hugh, of course), and when he came to Julia, he leaned down and said, "Write to me, won't you, Julia. I'll picture you at your desk with Patchy-cat curled up on it, watching you. And keep on telling your stories. If Maisie won't listen, remember Mama always wants to hear them."

So then Julia gave him her letter that he was to read on the train, and he took out his wallet and put it away safe. Then he put his arms around Mama and kissed her a long goodbye, then went up the train steps with his bag. And Julia got terrifically excited and began hopping up and down screaming, *"Goodbye, Daddy—goodbye—goodbye—goodbye!"* so piercingly that Aunt Alex put her hands to her ears. "Oh, Julia, Julia—that will do!" even though there were lots of other children shouting goodbye just as loud.

Now there was Daddy at the window, smiling at them and nodding and waving, and then he sat down and just looked at them, at Mama and Greg and Julia. Mama, when the train began moving, walked along beside the window, blowing kisses. And when the train gathered speed she stood there, left behind, her hands at her mouth, palms together. Greg ran to keep up, with Julia chasing after as fast as she could. But soon the train outdistanced them and Daddy was gone.

6

Dear Father

July 26

Dear Father   That Bob and Greg banged a nail in some sooet on the oak tree and the oak tree was bleeding and I cried and they made fun of me and said I was silly but the oak tree was hurt if it bled. The sooet was for the birds. *Did it hurt?*

August 5

Dear Father   Things are fixd. Mr. Woolerd saw Greg mixing the sement pouder and came over and asked about it and so Greg said about the crak and so Mr. Woolerd banged on the wawk with a big hamer and dug up the place and got out the root that was

pushing up and then they put in the sement and then
he got up on the roof and then he came in and got at
the drips. And Mama had a fit. But Mr. Woolerd is nice
and didnt mind a bit. I showd him my desk and he put
his hand on it and slid it around and said he couldnt
do better. Not even Mr. Wollerd!!!

August 16
Dear Father   You said in your letter you didn't
ever see the grinling. Or I mean ever know he was
there but I think its because your big and Gregs bigger
than it is so the grinling stays under the vines. At night.
You said about helping Mama and I do and I have to
dust Felony. In case Aunt Alex asks to see her. I dont
like Felony.

August 28
Dear Father   Maisie dosnt like dolls. But she keeps
loking at Felony. Its so funny the way she keeps looking at her. She says Im meen to keep her way under
the desk. But she hates dolls so its funny. She thinks
a desk is sily and hates desks. Its like scool. But it isnt
like scool a bit. Its my desk and its big with all my
things and smooth drawers. And lots of room. I like
riting here.

September 8

Dear Father   I was in the bathroom and Gramma said I cam out to soon but I was throo but she said I couldnt be it was to fast. It was for more than to tinkl and I had to go back and sit there. For nothing. I was so mad!

———◆———

September 17

Dear Father   Maisie loks at Felony so much. So I said she coud take her and she got so mad. I dont know why but she wont speek to me she said everbody knows she hates dolls so I went over and calld but she only lookd out the door.

———◆———

September 29

Dear Father   Patchy is sitting on my desk and he always sits on my desk in the sun when I am riting he is so beatiful. I was mad at him he got a bird and so I throo the bird down because I was afraid it wasnt ded and Greg and Bob said I was sily. But if it wasnt ded!!! But it was and Maisie and me had a funral for it and we sang and said a pryr and put a name on a card for it and stuk it in the grownd and Patchycat came and lookd.

———◆———

October 5

Dear Father   So now you are in Ingland. And you will fly over the kings that are stupid and wickid. Uncle Hugh told Greg and me about the wikid and stupid kings that startd the war. Well maybe you are in Frans. I get mixed up. Did you know the grinling is still in the garden? Do you think he woud hurt me?

———◆———

7

The Grinling in the Garden

It was something Julia had to decide—whether the grinling would do anything, *really,* if she went into the garden in the dark. The thing was, she couldn't stand having Felony there under the desk anymore.

Mama had come in and given Julia's floor a good sweeping and polishing with the mop. And she put Felony down with her back to the french door again and leaning against the front leg of the desk. And when Julia woke up in the night and saw her there in the bright October moonlight, with the light shining across the floor, she noticed that Felony's eyes weren't shining in reflection. She got up and went over and looked at Felony's face. And there were no eyes, only two black holes.

She knew what had happened. The eyes had come loose and fallen back in Felony's head. And when she picked her up, sure enough, she could hear them rattling around inside. She had explored under Felony's wig where there was an open place and, looking down inside, saw that her eyes were all in one piece, two glass balls with a bar in the middle. And the bar was attached to the inside of her head with a piece of glue that must have cracked, so that the eyes had fallen.

She couldn't bear to think of Felony with those two dark, empty holes in her face. She opened the door and looked into the garden, all black shadows and patches of silver the way it had been after Aunt Alex and Uncle Hugh's party before Daddy went away.

Yes, Felony would be happy out there among the leaves, way back in the bushes where the birds hopped in and out. But nobody must know or they'd say Felony must come back in. And Julia didn't want her to come back in. Maisie wouldn't take her, so she must have another home.

Julia stared into the darkness and knew she couldn't steal out there and hide Felony. Not now, not with the grinling waiting. But during the day sometime, when no one was around—when Greg was over with Bob, and Mama was at work—she would find the right place. No matter what, she *would* hide Felony. And Felony would be lots happier out there in the garden, maybe over under the rose geranium that grew very

thick against the fence and smelled so good, than in
here getting dusty under the desk.

October 20

Dear Father   Somthing funny about Felony. Her
eyes fell down in her hed and I didnt like it so she has
a new home. I hope she is hapy. She can hear the birds
and be by them. I hope she is frens with the grinling
and he likes her. I think she is alright. Maisie said whair
is Felony when she was over to play and I said she has
a new home. And Maisie didnt say anything. Then she
said did you give her to sombody. And I said no. But
maybe I gave her to the grinling.

Mama, too, wanted to know where Felony was, so
Julia said she was a princess hiding from the wicked
troll, but that she was *perfectly safe.* Mama wasn't to
worry.

"Probably stuffed away at the back of some closet,"
said Mama. "But, Julia, just in case Aunt Alex and
Uncle Hugh should come by—" when here came
Gramma at the front door. And she and Mama got
into such a discussion about something, as they so
often did, that Mama seemed to forget all about Felony.

In the mysterious light of evening, Julia called to
Maisie,

Come out, come out,
Wherever you be,
Come out from under
The bumblebee tree—

and Maisie came running from somewhere, Julia couldn't tell from where because she had her eyes covered. And Maisie shouted at Julia, "You're supposed to yell 'Ollie, ollie, oxen free,' not that about a bumblebee tree. Whoever heard of a bumblebee tree! There is no such thing. You're silly."

"I am not silly. There's a tree with flowers all over it in the summer and it's full of bumblebees and Uncle Hugh calls it the bumblebee tree."

"Then *he's* silly!"

"Don't you call my Uncle Hugh silly," blazed Julia.

"Silly, silly, silly old Uncle Hugh!" shrieked thin little Maisie, her two long dark pigtails flying out behind her as she streaked for home. "*Stupid* old Uncle Hugh!"

Julia raced after her, full of wrath, but Maisie made it up the front steps of her house, snatched open the front door, and banged it closed behind her a second before Julia got there.

But the odd thing was that half an hour later, when it was dark and Julia had gone into her own house and was setting the table, she heard Mrs. Woollard calling, out on their porch, "Mai-ai-zeeee! Dinnertime!" and after a little, Mrs. Woollard came to the door asking for Maisie.

"But she's home, Mrs. Woollard. We were playing hide-and-seek over here, and she said Uncle Hugh was silly for calling one of the trees a bumblebee tree, so I chased her up on your front porch and she got inside just in time."

"*Well,*" said Mrs. Woollard, "she's not there now."

"Maybe the grinling got her," said Julia with satisfaction. She certainly hoped it had, not to finish Maisie off, but just to give her a good hard scare. Serve her right!

"And what is the grinling, may I ask?" demanded Mrs. Woollard.

"It lives in our garden and it gets bad children," said Julia.

"Oh, rubbish!" cried Mrs. Woollard, turning to go home again. "You and your stories. Maisie's likely in the house this very minute."

And she must have been, because Mrs. Woollard didn't come back asking for Maisie, and the next day there she was, just as wiry and solemn and neat as ever, wanting Julia to come out and play.

"Where were you last night, Maisie Woollard, when your mother was calling all over the place for you?"

"No place," said Maisie.

"Well, why didn't you come when she called?"

"Because," said Maisie. "None o' your business."

8

Be Still, Little Lady

Now it was Saturday, and late in the afternoon Mama asked Julia and Maisie if they would go along to the baker's and get one of those wonderful, crusty loaves of bread Mr. Juniper baked every morning. The loaves were made double, and when Mrs. Juniper at the counter broke one half away from the other, the break was all delicious-smelling and soft and fluffy. And it was the hardest thing, on the way home, to keep from taking little nips out of the soft part.

In fact, when Julia and Maisie peeked into the bag and took sniffs of the fresh-baked bread, they couldn't keep from taking one or two nips, then one or two more. But finally Julia was overcome with guilt.

"Golly, what will Mama say? It looks like a mouse has been at it."

"No, a *rat!*" shrieked Maisie, and they both screamed with laughter, and ran into the playground of their school, where the rings were and the acting bar and the swings. Maisie always went for the swings, but Julia ran over to the rings.

She tossed down the bread and struggled as usual to shinny up the slanting metal pole until she could get high enough to reach out for a ring. She kept sliding down, so she rubbed her hands in the dust and had another try. This time she managed to get up high enough to capture the end ring one of the bigger kids had left swinging back and forth. Now she launched herself into space and, at the top of her swing, grasped the next ring.

Away she went, breathless with delight and excitement, swinging in great arcs from ring to ring, along the whole length of them, until her arms could take no more. But it was glorious. There was nothing more thrilling than to go rocketing through the air, far above the ground, free as a bird. And there was always the little edge of scarey anxiousness, because she was so high up for her size, that she just might not get the next ring. Then she would have to drop off and her feet would burn, or hang by one arm and have another try for that next ring on its second swing back.

But she had caught every single one on the first go.

Just wait till Uncle Hugh came over with her and she would show him how she could swing the whole length of the rings! She'd never done that before.

She grasped hold of the slanting pole at the other end and slid down. Now for the acting bar. Luckily, she remembered the bread and threw it down over on the other side of the playground near the bars.

"C'mon, Maisie," she yelled. "Come'n try again— maybe you'll like it this time."

She got up on the box under the highest bar of all, reached up with both hands, turned herself upside down, and slid both legs, as far as her behind, over the shiny, slick bar until she was sitting on it. This was called "skinning the rabbit."

"Maisie—Maisie—watch me!" she shrieked, and with one leg hooked over, she whirled and whirled as if she were a wheel and the bar were an axle. Then she stopped to see if Maisie had been watching, and to enjoy Maisie's envy of her skill.

But Maisie was on her way over to the gate and turned only to yell back, "You can stay by yourself. I gotta go home," and she trotted away down the street, never looking back once.

"Oh, phoo, phoo," said Julia to herself. "Gotta go home—gotta go home," and over she went, whirling and whirling, then sat on top of the bar again and dropped over with both legs together instead of with one of them hooked. Next she skinned the rabbit again and went on whirling.

Oh, but she must have been going too fast, because when she swung to the top for the sixth or seventh time, her hands slipped, she flew through the air, saw the tops of the trees flash in an arc, then the hard black surface of the playground come whizzing toward her —and nothing more.

She came to herself as if she were rising out of depth after depth of darkness, of nothingness—and there was something going *creak-creak, creak-creak, creak-creak.* Her head throbbed, and her cheek. Fearfully she opened her eyes and saw a room she did not know and had a feeling of dim light and sickening hotness. She tried to say something—but to whom? And the *creak-creak, creak-creak* went on and on.

She could only close her eyes. She couldn't possibly get up. Perhaps this way, if she waited and didn't move, she would get back somehow to Mama and Greg, and to her own house. She hadn't the least idea where she was or what had happened.

It seemed to Julia that she and her father were in the garden. Only it was puzzling, because the garden was much, much bigger than it had ever been—more like a park. And they were climbing a little narrow path up through oaks and pines and eucalyptus. Up and up they went, until Bob's house and Maisie's and her own vanished, and all the other houses. And when Julia turned and looked back, they were high in the Berkeley hills, and there was Berkeley spread out beneath them, and the bay and San Francisco beyond. Why, they were way, way up! How had they gotten so far so fast?

They were walking up the path hand in hand, and Daddy was telling her about when he was a boy in England. He'd loved to play a game called soccer. And Daddy's soccer shoes were too small, so that they hurt him, but his parents couldn't afford to get him a new pair.

So he found a job delivering groceries and he had to get up awfully early in the morning, sometimes before it was light, to get together everything on his lists and put it all in a wagon. Then he walked all over town, delivering. But when he'd saved up enough money for the soccer shoes, his mother told him how sorry she was, but that she needed the money to buy their own groceries because they were having such a hard time. And so Daddy didn't get his soccer shoes after all.

Julia burst into tears. "Mean—mean—mean!" she sobbed. She could hardly bear it. "That wasn't right— she had no right to take your money!"

"Oh, but they needed it, Julia, they had to have it. Even that little bit. But never mind. I worked and saved up some more, and finally I did get those soccer shoes—"

Presently Julia had to walk in front of him because

the path got so steep and narrow, with a big drop over the side. And when they came to a sharp turn, Daddy put his hand on Julia's head.

"Now, Julia," he said, "you must go back or Mama will be worried. Go back like a good girl. I have to go on alone."

"No, I don't want to go back by myself. Take me with you—please. Let me go too."

"Julia," said Daddy, and there was a certain tone in his voice that she knew, "there's no use making a fuss. You must go back at once. I've brought you much too far as it is." And he leaned down and swung her up, gave her a good hug and kiss, and held her for a moment. "Remember one thing," he said. "Remember to tell Mama to go through my papers."

"I will," she promised. "Mama must go through your papers. What does that mean?"

But he only smiled without answering. Then he was the one who turned away first; and he went around the curve in the path where a big rock hid him from sight. She stood there, waiting to see him again, farther along. There he was! They waved and blew each other kisses, and then Daddy, when he was away off (but how could he have gotten so far in such a short time?), went around another turn in the path and she saw him no more.

But now, what a shock. For when she started down, she saw that there was no Berkeley lying at the foot of the hills. San Francisco Bay was gone, and San Francisco and the Golden Gate, too, had vanished—or had never been. There was nothing but hills, and more and more of them, stretching away in every direction as far as she could see. There were no pine woods, nor oaks and eucalyptus, the woods she and her father had climbed through. There were no trees at all, just smooth, bare, golden brown hills. Not an animal. Not a bird. And one hill was exactly like another, and when she turned to look where she and Daddy had been, it was all just like everything else, so that she had no idea which way to go.

But, wait—it seemed to her that she could hear, very faintly, someone calling her. "Ju-u-li-aaa—Ju-u-li-aaa!" That was Mama. She knew it was Mama! And then *"Jule! Hey, Jule!"* That was Greg.

"Mama!" she shouted in terror. *"Greg—Greg!"*

She ran blunderingly along with hot tears streaming down her face, and no matter what path she took, it made no difference, for every path was exactly like every other. Sometimes there would be more of the big boulders like the one at the bend where her father had gone on ahead. And because tears were blurring her sight, she ran into one of them and her cheek ached deep inside and the flesh burned where she had scraped it. *"Mama—Mama—Mama—!"*

"Be still, little lady," said a voice. "Just you be still now—stop thrashing around." Something cool was put against her burning, hurting cheek, and when she opened her eyes, there was a soft, round, wrinkled face like a large pudding leaning over and smiling and nodding. "Be still—you'll be just fine." There was a moment of silence while the little black eyes in the round pudding face gazed at her. "My," said the old woman to whom the face belonged, "my, my, but that's quite a cheek you have."

Julia put her hand up and could scarcely believe that this cheek was hers, for it was all bulged out and hot and lumpy. She began sobbing to herself out of fright and the terribly empty feeling of lostness that was still within her. She sat up and looked around—but how dizzy she was, and how her head ached!

She was in a room filled with all sorts of old over-stuffed furniture, much too much furniture. The room was suffocating, with not a door nor a window open, yet the old woman had on a big, thick sweater. The house smelled of something Julia could not put a name to, something like onions but with a queer edge to it she couldn't abide. It caught at the back of her throat.

She turned to the windows alongside the couch where she'd been lying. And it was dark outside.

Oh, but it couldn't be—it couldn't possibly be dark already. Up in the hills, it—but that wasn't the time she wanted. *What did she want?* She couldn't think—she was all muddled and confused. She and Maisie—or was that some other day? But it couldn't be night. She *knew* that. Because Mama would be too worried; she'd be frantic with worry that Julia wasn't home yet. No, no—not night! Please, not night.

"Where am I? What's happened—?"

Now the old woman tried to push her down again, and to cover her with a blanket. A blanket—in this sickeningly hot room! "Just lie quiet, little lady, and Brother will soon be back. He had to go out and do a bit of shopping, but he'll be back soon and then we'll have a nice dinner, just the three of us. He said you were to stay quiet right here and that I mustn't let you out—"

"But I have to go home!" shouted Julia, as if the old woman were deaf, and she struggled out from under the grasping hands, tore herself away, and ran across the room. The door on the opposite side led into a hallway, but when she tried the big door at the end that would open onto the front porch, she found it was locked.

She fumbled with the knob, turned and yanked at it, tried to turn the little button underneath that would unlock the door from the inside, but couldn't move it. No amount of turning and pulling did the least good. Now, with the old lady calling anxiously to her to "stay until Brother comes," she ran across what seemed to be another sitting room stuffed with furniture, and back through the house to the kitchen. But the kitchen door too was locked. And no window could be budged. All of them were stuck fast with paint that had dried hard long ago.

"Let me phone," cried Julia to the old woman. "Where is the phone?"

"We don't have one. We've never needed one," came the old woman's reply from the room where Julia had been lying on the couch.

"Mama—Mama!" Julia ran through the house trying all the windows, stumbled upstairs, and, at one of them in a front bedroom, looked down and saw Greg and Mama at the corner under a streetlamp, talking and pointing here and there as though deciding where to hunt next.

Julia pounded on the window and screamed, and a great crack sprang across it, sparkling like a small lightning as the gleam from the streetlamp caught its flight. She stared at the crack in horror, then saw Mama and Greg separate and go in opposite directions along the street that ran at right angles to the one this big old house stood on.

Desperately she ran downstairs to beg to be let out, and now the old woman offered her some crumbling, ancient cookies in a grease-stained box.

"No, no, there's no leaving the house," she said in answer to Julia's pleading. "Have something to eat, little lady, then you'll feel better. Come and lie down. You need to lie down—no use crying and calling. I promised Brother I would keep you safe until he came back, and so I've locked us up all nice and cozy. Come and sit down now, and tell me about yourself. What's your name and what have you—?"

Julia swept out her arm and knocked the box of moldy cookies clear across the hall, and they hit the blurred mirror hanging there that had a silvery blot in the middle of it, and fell out of the box and made a mess of crumbs on the carpet. The old lady stood there shaking her big head back and forth, back and forth. She seemed appalled.

"That wasn't nice at all, little lady. You are a naughty girl. That was a wicked waste. Well, so I shall go sit by myself, and you shall stay here and clean up the crumbs. Clean them all up now, and put them in the box."

Off she went into the room where the couch was, and presently there was a creaking as of a rocking chair, *creak-creak, creak-creak, creak-creak.* Julia sank down at the foot of the stairs and cried. What could she do now? Nothing—nothing. Never had she felt so sick and hollow with despair.

She had no idea how long it was she stayed there crying to herself. She couldn't even begin to imagine what had happened to her. How had she gotten from the hills into this big house? Had she and Maisie gone up alone? But they wouldn't—that was a long, long way. No, there was the playground. And she saw Maisie going across it toward the gate, saying she had to

go home. And then—then what happened? Julia had whirled and whirled on the acting bar, then flown through the air and come down on the hard, dusty blackness—and that was all. But there was something more, something about the hills. What could it be? And if she *had* gone up there, when had it been? And why had she gone?

9

Fame

She must have fallen asleep, because when she opened her eyes—again, for just a breath, she had no idea where she was. She heard footsteps on the porch, then a key was turned in the lock, the door was opened, and the naked light bulb hanging from the ceiling blazed on.

"*Mama!* Oh, Mama, Mama!" She couldn't believe it. She had never expected to see Mama and Greg again. But there they were, standing with a policeman and someone tall and bent and gray with a flat cap on. And she was at once wrapped around in a big hug in Mama's winter coat that smelled like her, nothing at all like Aunt Alex's perfume—no, much, much better.

This was it. This was what she wanted. Mama smelled cool and fresh and clean after the horrible odor of the house, the hot, oniony, closed-up, dusty odor, as if no one had opened a door or a window in a hundred years.

"Julia, your face—your face!" Mama had gotten down on one knee to take Julia in her arms, and had drawn back to look at her. "What's happened—what did you do to yourself? Why, it looks as if someone has hit you—!"

"Some*thing* hit me," shouted Julia. She had to shout, she was so relieved and excited and joyous. "Some*thing*—that old playground! I was on the acting bar and I flew off. Where's Maisie? Didn't she tell you I was at the playground?"

"Of course she did," said Greg impatiently. "Don't you s'pose we asked her? First thing. She said she left you there, and we found the loaf of bread." There it was in Greg's hand, the white bag all rumpled and dirty. "And then Mom and I called and called and called, up one street and down another—"

"I know—I know! I saw you. I was upstairs and I *saw* you. You were standing under the streetlamp over there on the corner, pointing and talking away, and I screamed at you and I banged on the window so hard it cracked, but you wouldn't look up, so I ran downstairs again and I couldn't get out because she wouldn't let me out—the old lady wouldn't—"

"The window," said the tall gray man, all stooped

over at the shoulders, still with his flat cap on and an old gray sweater like his sister's, and carrying a bag of groceries. "The window, cracked, you say—ah, that will have to be paid for—" But it was strange, the way he didn't look at Mama, or at anyone really. He kept staring around past people, and a lot of the time at the carpet, with the cookies spilled in a pile of crumbs on it with a good bit of scattering. He seemed puzzled by this sight.

"But why did you shut the child up?" demanded the policeman.

"I couldn't get out," said Julia breathlessly. "I tried —I tried to get out this door and the back door but the old woman had them all locked, and she said she'd promised Brother she'd keep me here until he got back. And I ran to all the windows but I couldn't open a single one, downstairs or upstairs. And they don't have a phone. There wasn't any way I could do anything—" Again the wave of hopeless despair washed over her, as sharp as she'd felt it before, sickening, even with Mama and Greg right here in front of her, the hopelessness of probably being imprisoned in this house forever.

Mama rose up. "*Why,*" she said, her voice deep and trembling with anger, "*why* would you lock this child in, when my son and I have been calling all over the neighborhood for the last hour, and I had to get a policeman—?"

"But I didn't hear you," said the gray man, still not

looking at her, and shaking his head. "As I told you outside, I've been at the grocer's for the last hour or so —"

"But your sister must have heard—"

"Oh, I *did,* " said the old lady. "Yes, yes, I did—but I promised Brother I'd keep the child here. I *promised* him—so there was nothing I could do."

"But why did you lock Julia up?" persisted Mama, grasping the gray man by the arm. "You still haven't answered."

"Because," he said, "I wanted to be here. My sister, you see, isn't very good at business matters—"

"At *bus*iness matters!" exploded the policeman. "*What* business matters?"

"Why, the reward, of course," said Brother, looking all around as though searching for something, and sounding astonished. "Surely a reward is in order. After all, a person's child—and there she lay, unconscious"—here he lifted an arm, stiffly, like a bad actor—"and would have remained so. But I saw her from an upstairs window, lying on the playground, and I went out and brought her over here and put her on the couch where my sister put hot and cold cloths on her face. Perhaps we saved her life—"

"Saved her life—rubbish!" exclaimed the policeman. "You did the only thing any humane person *would* have done. Only you should have called a doctor. And when she came to, she'd have been able to go home at once if you'd had a grain of sense. As it was, her mother has been beside herself, especially when it got dark. For locking the child up, I have a good mind to take you down to the police station—"

The old woman let out a wail of dismay.

"Oh, no, no, please!" said Mama. "Here—" and she opened her purse and began rooting around, found her wallet, and got out a bill. "It's all I have with me," she said, "and if the windowpane costs more—let me know. And I thank you for taking care of Julia."

But the policeman laid a firm hand over hers. "Indeed not," he said. "That pane would never have gotten cracked if Julia hadn't been locked up. She must have been out of her mind with fright—it's a wonder she didn't smash it. As for you, Mr. Berenda, you can thank your stars I'm not having you down to the station. Just don't go locking anyone else up, hoping for a reward. And now I think we'd better get this child home at once so she can go to bed."

"Golly," said Greg, "you look *awful.*"

Julia was lying in state in Mama's bed, propped up with pillows. She had been carried home by the policeman, whose name was Officer Stanton. Patchy-cat lay curled at her feet, and she was having her favorite supper she always had when she wasn't feeling good: bread broken up in hot milk, the bread buttered, and brown sugar and raisins sprinkled over. Her cheek still burned and her head still hurt. But she was home, with Patchy-cat rumbling against her feet.

"Get me the mirror—let me look."

So Greg got the mirror, and she gazed at herself. She could hardly believe this was the Julia she knew. Why, she looked absolutely fierce. Her cheek was swollen as big as an apple, and it was all scratched and red, with long scratches as if she'd slid on gravel when she landed.

And her eye on that side was black, and the other was darkish and coming along for black, both of them looking out at her from under a tangled mop of reddish brown hair. But then, unless it was freshly combed, it usually was a mop. "You live too hard, Julia," Mama would say.

The doctor had come (he was just home from his office, and his house was only two blocks away). He said that Julia was surely not concussed. That is, cracked in the head, and she could tell this was supposed to be his little joke because of the sparkle in his eye when she looked up at him.

"You mean my head bone?"

"Your skull, Jule—your skull, not your head bone," said Greg scornfully.

"Then it's definitely not cracked, you think, Dr. Silverman?" asked Mama anxiously.

"The headache would be severe if it were. Do you have a bad headache, Julia?"

"Not bad—just a little."

"But I think," said Dr. Silverman, "that she should meet me at the hospital tomorrow morning and we'll have an X ray, just to be certain. Of course children's bones are softer than the brittle old grown-ups' are, and don't break as easily. I think you're going to be just fine, Julia. Not to worry."

So she didn't worry, and he left after talking to Mama in the living room for a few minutes. Then there was the doorbell again, and Greg and Mama brought in Mr. and Mrs. Woollard and Maisie. Maisie sat on the edge of the bed and stared at Julia, while her mother and father stood gravely at the foot.

"Do sit down, Mrs. Woollard," said Mama. "Greg, bring over a chair and go get one for Mr. Woollard. Will you have some coffee?"

"Well, we've already had our—but, yes, that would be very nice, thank you," said Mrs. Woollard so politely, like company, you'd never imagine she'd drop over any Saturday or Sunday to borrow an egg or tell Mama some bit of neighborhood gossip.

She sat down and surveyed Julia. "Child, the *look* of you!" she said, her large ivory teeth giving a click, a thing they often did, which Julia had never been able to understand. "What is your mother to do with you? I've never seen such a young one for getting into trouble."

"But I couldn't help it, Mrs. Woollard. I was only doing my stunts on the acting bar."

"Yes, but it was the high one, Julia," pointed out Maisie, who never let anything pass. "And you shouldn't have *been* on the high one. You know what your mother said about the high one, that it's dangerous. I heard her."

"Yes," said Mrs. Woollard. "There is that, Julia. That about the high one. But you've always been the same, I'm told. Never will listen. I remember the bicycle. Greg's bike, and your poor aunt right in the path. Now our Maisie, she's never been one to—"

But here came more voices, and Mama brought in Bob and his mother and father, and Greg got more chairs, and they sat there studying Julia's face in surprise. Then they were all served coffee except the children, but everyone had cookies Mama had made that very afternoon while Julia and Maisie were away at the baker's—a big batch of them, as if she'd known they'd be needed for this special occasion. Now they all began laughing and talking at once, asking Julia what it had felt like to be locked up in that old house, not knowing why, and did her face hurt and did she know she had two beauties of black eyes?

My, it's like a party, thought Julia, amazed, and all because of me.

So then she told the whole story, just the way she'd told Mama and Greg and the policeman, only in much more detail, just how she'd felt when she discovered it was night, and how the house smelled, and about the moldy cookies and how she'd thrown them at the mirror, and about seeing Mama and Greg down at the corner and how she was sure she'd never see them again after they'd walked away in the darkness.

All the time she was telling, she was aware of Maisie sitting there—not looking at Julia, but down at the bed and making patterns on the bedspread with her finger. Then Mr. Woollard spoke up for the first time and said, what was this about Julia smashing a window.

"No, she didn't, Mr. Woollard," said Greg loudly, having to make himself heard over everyone exclaiming at Julia smashing a window. "She didn't—she just cracked it, when she saw Mom and me. She banged on it, and it cracked. But I'd have smashed it. I'd never have stayed in that place for a second. Why didn't you smash it, Jule? When you were upstairs and saw us? We'd have heard it break and you could have shouted at us. No sense in staying with just that old lady to keep you there."

Everybody was talking again, and Julia was thinking: Why, she couldn't have broken it! To break a window was an awful thing. Even locked up, scared as she was, she'd felt a shock go through her when she saw that big windowpane crack right across. Yes, but if she'd kept *on* being locked up—what then?

"The policeman didn't want me to pay for it," said Mama. "Officer Stanton. He made me put my money back. But I felt I should pay for the damage my child had done. Yes, yes, I know," she said when everyone began telling her that she was wrong, and just why she was. "But you see, those two old people aren't quite right in the head anymore, and their neighbors agree —especially about old Mr. Berenda. Can't you tell? They've been living to themselves in that house for so long, hardly ever seeing a soul, that I have an idea they're really odd by now. And maybe they don't have very much money, which is why Mr. Berenda thought about a reward—"

Well, what a discussion there was then, everyone saying that Mama was being far too kindhearted, and that the Berendas weren't all that peculiar, and that Mr. Berenda had done a very heartless thing, staying away all that time at the grocery store not knowing how Julia was, nor what Mama must be feeling and thinking.

Then they all got up to go, and Maisie was the last one out. She turned at the door.

"I'm really famous, aren't I, Maisie?" said Julia in wonderment.

"You sure look terrible," answered Maisie. "I'm glad *I* don't look like you."

"Yes, but *I'm* going to have an X ray. I'll bet *you* never had an X ray."

"Well, *I* wouldn't want one. I bet anything it hurts. You wait and see."

10

Julia and
Uncle Hugh

Julia came straggling home from a deserted stable down the street, where some older kids were putting on a play.

She'd begged to be in other plays they'd put on, and they had let her—just in little parts. The first time, she'd been a ghost in a sheet Mama had given her because it was past mending. Then there were flowers in the next play, so she'd offered to be a lily and came along to the stable in her sheet again, with a stick wrapped in orange crepe paper tied to her head for the lily's stamen.

Next, she was to be the West Wind, and Mama helped her paint wavy blue lines on the sheet to show how the wind blew. The kids hadn't understood this until she'd explained to them that the lines meant the wind was blowing. They just barely let her in.

This time, when she turned up at the stable in her grubby, wrinkled old sheet to be the Sea, making use of the wavy blue lines, they all groaned. And when they saw her awful face, they made believe they were going to sick up their lunches and said she had to go on away. They couldn't stand looking at her, they said. And they were all bored with that old sheet and didn't want ever to see her in it again.

Mean, mean, she thought, going back home. After all, it didn't make them sick to look at horrible Halloween masks that were lots worse than her face. They just didn't want her around—that was it.

As she made her way toward Maisie's house, holding up the dirty, torn edges of the sheet so she wouldn't stumble over it, she saw Mr. Berenda coming back from the grocery store with another big bagful of groceries.

"Hello, Mr. Berenda," she called, good and loud in case he couldn't hear very well. He turned and stared at her over his groceries as if she were a stranger. "It's me, Julia Redfern—don't you remember?" she shouted, and started running so that he wouldn't get away before she could reach him. "I had my X rays and it wasn't *any*thing, Mr. Berenda. They didn't hurt a bit like Maisie said they would. All it was was a lot of pictures, and I saw my skull bone without any meat on it, and there were two big holes for eyes, and a hole for my nose, and all my teeth showed at once, but no crack in my head," and she threw back her sheet so that he could see she had a whole, uncracked skull.

He just stood there, his eyes wide as if he was frightened, and never said a word. Julia couldn't imagine what he was thinking—except, maybe about the policeman and the police station? Certainly he didn't look a bit happy!

Then all at once he shifted his bag of groceries to the other arm and made off as fast as he could across the street. She had an idea he didn't want to hear anything more about her skull bone, or about anything at all to do with her, Julia Caroline Redfern. She almost thought, in fact, that he never wanted to see her again, he went off so fast.

Feeling rather low because nobody seemed to want to see her, she turned along Maisie's front walk remembering how she'd been famous once, such a short time ago, with everybody crowding into Mama's bedroom to hear all about her adventures. Maybe Maisie wouldn't want to see her either. She rang the bell. No answer, no matter how long she rang and rang. So she went down the stairs and around the house. And there was Mrs. Woollard in the backyard, leaning over and looking into the window of a little gardening shed where they stored odds and ends.

As Julia came toward her, Mrs. Woollard looked up, put her finger to her lips as if to hush Julia from saying anything, then beckoned to her to come and look too.

Julia went and stood beside Mrs. Woollard and looked in.

She could scarcely believe what she saw. For there was Maisie with her back to them, sitting on a box in the rays of the afternoon sun shining in the window at the rear of the shed. She was holding something in her arms and singing to it, and when she turned a little, Julia recognized Felony's head. Felony was, of course, being held with her face toward Maisie, and Julia could see that Felony's eyes were in their eye sockets again where they belonged.

Julia's mouth opened. It was the last thing she would ever have expected to see in the Woollard's gardening shed, Maisie singing to the rescued Felony. And rocking Felony in her arms as if she loved her!

"But—" began Julia, and felt Mrs. Woollard's hand pressing her arm to silence her.

"Sh-sh! Go and wait at the front steps," Mrs. Woollard whispered in her ear. "I'll be there presently."

So Julia ran up front and waited, and in a little while here came Mrs. Woollard by herself carrying Felony, and Julia could tell by the red spots in her cheeks that she was seething with indignation. "Julia Redfern," she said, "what did you mean by hiding this beautiful, expensive doll in your garden? Maisie said you put it out there because you don't like it and don't want it anymore. Why, of all the shameful things, after your aunt and uncle spending all that money! And there's

Maisie, after getting the doll's eyes back in place and gluing them, sitting out there in that shed this minute, crying and carrying on like I don't know what. Now you take it right back home with you this instant, and don't you *ever* do such a wicked thing again.''

"Oh, but, Mrs. Woollard, please don't make me. If Maisie wants it—''

"If Maisie wants a doll, we'll get it for her. Only she's always said she can't stand them. Now run along home with you. Your aunt and uncle are there—just came a little while ago, so thank heaven they don't need to ask you where your doll is.''

Julia looked across the street and there was Aunt Alex and Uncle Hugh's car. She'd never noticed, thinking so hard about how nobody wanted to see her anymore.

Heavy of heart, and holding Felony by one arm, she came into the living room with her sheet dragging back from her shoulders. Aunt Alex was there by herself, sitting in the big chair this time and looking strangely disordered. When she saw Julia, she put her hand to her face and gave a gasp. Then she put both hands to her mouth as if she was starting to cry, and her eyes filled with tears.

"Where's Mama?'' But now Julia heard low voices in the bedroom, Uncle Hugh's, then Greg's, and then Mama's voice answering them. And the sound of Mama's somehow gave Julia a dreadful, anxious feeling. "What's the matter, Aunt Alex? Is there something—?"

"Oh, Julia—your mother told me about you, but I wasn't ready, not at all, for the way you—" and here she took her hands from her mouth and Julia saw that it was all sort of crushed up. "And that stupid doll!" Aunt Alex exclaimed suddenly in a shaking voice. "You don't really like it, do you, Julia? You never have. I could tell at the time—it's too big. Go and put it away, dear. Uncle Hugh wants to talk to you—"

"Aunt Alex. About Felony. Would you mind if Maisie had her? She loves Felony and would like awfully to have her. Only she wouldn't take her if I gave Felony to her—I know she wouldn't. So could maybe Uncle Hugh take her over and—?"

"Some other time, dear—some other time. But of course Maisie can have her. Hugh," and Aunt Alex looked up as Uncle Hugh came in from Mama's bedroom, "why don't you and Julia go for a walk? Don't you think that would be a good idea?" He nodded, his eyes fixed on Julia's face, as if the looks of her were too much for him. "Yes, I know," said Aunt Alex. "Isn't the poor child a sight! And right now, of all times, to have had *this* happen. Is she—is Celia—?" and Aunt Alex tilted her head toward Mama in the bedroom.

Uncle Hugh closed his eyes for an instant and drew a sharp breath. "Come on, Julia," and he held out his hand. "Leave the sheet and the doll behind. You wouldn't mind, would you, going for a little walk with me?"

"Oh, Uncle Hugh—" and Julia gave a hop for joy. "I know what we can do. You'll see." She would take Uncle Hugh to the playground and he could lift her up to the rings and she would show him how she could swing from one end of them to the other without a single miss. And he wouldn't be able to believe it, because she couldn't do it the last time he'd gone with her. But she clung to Felony. She wasn't—for anything —going to miss this chance of getting Felony over to Maisie's house to stay forever.

And when they got out on the front porch she explained to Uncle Hugh how matters stood. He nodded sadly and put his hand on her head and said if that was the way she wanted it, of course he would see what he could do.

So she slipped her hand into his, thinking he was sad because she didn't want Felony. They went over to Maisie's and agreed that Julia should stay out on the sidewalk, along a little way in case Maisie came to the door and wouldn't like Julia hearing what went on. She went clear down to the corner out of sight. And when Uncle Hugh finally came out of Maisie's walk and along the street toward Julia, he nodded as if everything had been successful.

"I was talking to Mrs. Woollard about it," he said,

"and trying to make her understand that there was no earthly use in your having a doll like that, something that was just a waste, when Maisie came up behind her mother and listened. Mrs. Woollard was saying she just couldn't take it, considering what it had cost. But Maisie put her hand up and touched her mother's arm, and Mrs. Woollard turned and looked down at her and something seemed to happen, just in that instant, without their saying anything. Because Mrs. Woollard gave in, right then. So now that's all right, isn't it, Julia?"

They walked in silence toward the playground, Julia steering Uncle Hugh, who seemed far away in his thoughts and not to be caring what direction they took. But when they got there, he didn't seem to want to watch Julia on the rings—at least not just then. He sat down on one of the benches and said he had something to tell her. She sat beside him, looking up at him, and he put his arm around her shoulder and drew her closer.

He heaved a sigh that seemed to come out of his depths. "Julia, you know your father's been flying over enemy territory and getting into air battles with the enemy. Well, your mother got a telegram a little while ago that his plane has been shot down."

"Has he been hurt?"

"I'm afraid he won't come back, Julia. That's why they sent the telegram."

Julia jumped up. "You mean he's been killed. No, he's all right, Uncle Hugh, he's all right! I thought about that—about somebody shooting his plane. And he was over a forest, and when the plane dropped, he fell into the trees and the branches caught him, and he climbed down. *That's the way it was*—"

"Oh, Julia, Julia—you must understand. It's no use making up your stories about this. He won't come back." And Uncle Hugh took her hands and tried to pull her over to him so that she could sit on his lap, but she wrenched away.

"Yes, he *will*—he *will*. He's all *right!*"

And they went on and on like this, Julia standing in front of Uncle Hugh while he tried to make her believe what must be believed. But she put her hands over her ears and wouldn't listen. And when he got up to go, she ran ahead to get to Mama first to tell her what had really happened about the plane coming down in the trees.

But, oddly enough, for some reason she didn't go right in to Mama. Mama came into Julia's room where she was lying on her bed telling herself her story all over again about how it had been when Daddy's plane went down, and she saw very clearly everything that was happening. Mama tried to make her understand what Uncle Hugh had said, and that a telegram wouldn't have been sent unless the people who'd sent it had known the truth. But Julia kept saying over and over that there'd been a mistake. "He's all *right*. He's all *right*, I tell you. He's all *right*."

And nobody could make her believe that he wasn't —that he would not come back.

11

Patchy

The next thing that happened was that, at last, the war ended. But everything was very quiet at Mama and Julia and Greg's house, though they could hear all the celebrating going on downtown.

Then Mama got the flu. Everyone seemed to be getting it at the same time clear across the country and this, Gramma said when she came over to take care of them, was what was called an epidemic. She wouldn't take Greg's bed when he offered it, but made herself a bed on the couch in the living room by folding a couple of blankets with a sheet inside and pushing the ends down under the cushion at the foot.

Julia would get up early and steal across the living

room, past where Gramma was asleep, to Mama's room to see how she was. Mostly she did nothing but turn—back and forth, back and forth, and groan because, she said, she felt so unspeakably wretched with every bone aching.

It seemed to take a long time for Mama to get well, longer than for most of the people Gramma had taken care of. And once Julia heard Gramma say to Uncle Hugh that she wondered if Mama really wanted to. But why wouldn't she? Julia asked herself, too scared and lost-feeling to ask Gramma what she meant. Was it because of Daddy? Was that it? But she couldn't ask. Mama had to get well. She *had* to.

Patchy-cat wouldn't leave her. Always he was curled up at the foot of Mama's bed, watching her, or asleep. And he wouldn't move. He would jump down only to go outside to do his business and to eat a little, then he'd come right back in to Mama. Once, in the beginning, when Gramma tried to shut him out because she didn't approve of a cat being on the bed of someone who was sick, he went around and around outside the house sending up the most melancholy wails.

"Oh, let him in, Mother," said Mama fretfully. "Please let him in. I want him here. He's such a comfort to me. I don't know why, but he is."

So Gramma finally let him into the bedroom, that confounded cat, and Patchy raced across the floor, his paws making a firm, quick thudding as if he were a little horse. When he was up on the bed again, he walked over to Mama, licked her tenderly on the chin, then settled down next to her as close as he could get. And you could hear him purring clear across the room while he watched her, blinking in such an ecstasy of happiness that Julia had to laugh. And even Mama, sick as she was, had to smile. But Gramma was not amused. A spoiled-rotten animal, that's what he was, she said.

One morning, very early, when Julia was fast asleep, she felt something soft and furry rubbing against her face, and then Patchy spoke in her ear. "Owr-rrr!" he said, hollow and strange-sounding and urgent. "Owwwrrr-rrr!" Julia blinked awake and there was Patchy with his face right up against hers and he was looking into her eyes. "Owww-rrrr!"

"What is it, Patchy? You want out?" And she got up and went over to the french doors, wondering why Patchy hadn't used his own little door at the back in the kitchen. But no, he didn't want to go out. When she turned to look at him, he was standing at her door into the hall with one front paw up. "Owwr-r-rr!" And he went into the hall, still looking at her.

Instantly Julia knew he wanted her to come with him, and she followed along behind him to Mama's room. For some reason her heart was beating quick and hard, and she was frightened and shivering when she went in. Mama lay very still. When Julia came to the side of the bed and leaned over, Mama's face seemed to her to be too white, and her mouth was open and she was breathing low and quick but you could barely hear her. Julia reached out a hand and touched her cheek, and the skin felt frighteningly cold and damp.

"Gramma!" cried Julia, stricken with terror. *"Gramma—Gramma—!"*

Instantly, it seemed, Gramma was there. She took Mama's hand in hers and felt her forehead.

"Celia," she said in a low, firm, reaching voice Julia had never heard from her before, "Celia, you must come back. It's Mother, and Julia's here. I know how you feel without Harry, but *you must come back.* Julia and Greg need you—I can't take care of them, I'm too old for them, and you know Alex wouldn't make the kind of mother they should have, no matter how much Hugh loves them. Celia—can you hear me? Do you hear what I say? *You must come back—"*

Julia and Gramma waited, and then Mama turned her head, very slowly, and opened her eyes. "It's all right," she said in a faint voice. "I hear—I'll try—" Then she closed her eyes again and she was smiling just the smallest bit, as if to tell them that she really would.

At once Gramma went to get another blanket, and after she'd put it over Mama, Patchy hopped right back up again and settled himself like a little sphinx, with his front feet together, facing Mama, his eyes on her face.

When Julia and Gramma went into the other room,

Julia told what had happened, how Patchy had come into her bedroom and waked her and taken her in to Mama. Gramma, in her flannel nightgown, was sitting on the couch listening, with Julia on the floor, knees drawn up and arms clasped around them, and she was still shivering, not with fright now but with the aftereffect of what had happened.

For a moment or two, after Julia had finished, Gramma didn't say anything. Then she shook her head. "I don't know," she said in an unsteady voice. "That cat—whoever would have thought—" and then her chin crumpled, and she put her hand to her face. "That silly cat," she said. "That silly, faithful old cat."

12

That Time Up in the Hills

Of course Dr. Silverman came by whenever he could, but what would they have done without Gramma? She was like a small steely spring that curled itself up strong every night while she slept, ready to be used hard the next day. She got up at seven and worked all day long, ordering Greg and Julia around, cleaning and shopping and cooking and washing and ironing and taking care of Mama, giving her bed baths and putting her into a fresh nightgown every morning because Mama got so damp when she was sickest. Nothing seemed to stop Gramma. She never seemed to get really tired. And she didn't even get the sniffles, let alone the flu.

"*I* know what the secret is, Mother," Mama said one afternoon when she was feeling better and sitting up in bed and Julia had just gotten home from school. "You need to be needed—that's it! Then you're at your best."

Gramma was standing in the doorway of the bedroom. "Well," she said, "I don't know if you're teasing me or not, Celia, but I expect that's true. I like to work hard. I like to get up in the morning and see my day all laid out ahead of me, with plenty to do." And she went off to get the tea tray with a pot of dark-colored tea the way the English like it, the pot sitting under a tea cozy to keep the tea hot, and a plate of buttered toast and a bowl of strawberry jam she had made. Julia brought in her milk and cookies, and they all sat there together and talked.

All at once Mama put down her cup and looked over at where Daddy had had his desk, which was in Greg's room now with the typewriter on it. "Where's that box of Harry's papers, Mother? I thought it was over there in the corner."

"Well, it was," said Gramma, "but I had to clean and it was in the way."

"But where is it—what did you do with it?"

"I put it in a closet—it's all right. It's in that big closet on the other side of Julia's room."

Daddy's papers. Julia took a drink of milk, but there was beginning to be an anxious feeling in her stomach.

What was it about his papers? And why should the words suddenly make her sharply unhappy? There was something she had to remember—that she'd promised faithfully she would remember, and now she saw her father, that time up in the hills. But what time, and what about it?

They were climbing the hills together, and they'd gotten to the top. He said he'd brought her too far, that Mama would be worried, and that she must go back. But she hadn't wanted to go back—she hadn't wanted to leave him. But he said he had to go on alone. Then he'd said something else.

"Julia!" exclaimed Mama. "What is it, child? Your eyes are so big—what are you staring at? You look like an owl!"

Julia came to. "Daddy said that you must go through his papers. He made me promise I would tell you." She stopped and frowned. "What does 'go through' his papers mean, exactly?"

"That I'm to sort them out to see what's there. But when did he say this? Not before he left or he'd have told *me,* not you."

"No, it was after he left."

"But I don't understand. When could—do you mean he wrote you this?"

Julia shook her head. "We were up in the hills and he went on by himself and turned and waved to me, then went around a curve in the path a long way off, and I didn't see him anymore. And there was nothing but hills and I was lost."

"Oh, it's only another one of her stories she's made up, Celia," said Gramma. "You know that. You can't pay any—"

"But I *do* pay attention," said Mama. "And why should she make up something she doesn't understand —going through a person's papers? Was it a dream, Julia?"

"May-be," said Julia slowly, trying to decide. "Maybe it was. When I opened my eyes, I was in that old, smelly house and there was that old woman's wrinkled face leaning over me—Mr. Berenda's sister. And it was so hot in there it made me sick."

Mama leaned forward. There was silence in the room for a moment, and when she spoke there was urgency in her voice. "Mother, I must have that box of Harry's papers. I must go through them."

"Just because of what Julia's said?" cried Gramma in astonishment. "Why, that's ridiculous!"

"No, it's *not* ridiculous. Harry was writing all during those last three days he was at home, when he was supposed to be doing other things. He couldn't seem to stop. Now please, where is that box?"

Gramma gave a scornful, impatient little sniff, and said "Tchk!" but she got up and went out. And presently Julia and Mama heard doors opening and being banged closed at the other end of the house.

"Go and see what's the matter, Julia."

So Julia went to find Gramma, and there she was out in the kitchen, looking terribly upset. "What are *you* out here for?" she demanded.

"Gramma, can't you find the box?"

"I just can't seem to remember—" and she brushed past Julia and went back to Mama's bedroom. "Celia," she said abruptly, "it's simply a lot of foolishness to think some dream of Julia's has to be paid attention to right this minute. I cleared out your room, and I put everything—"

"Mother," said Mama in a deadly level voice, "you didn't throw those papers of Harry's away by any chance, did you?"

Gramma looked shocked and intensely indignant, both at once. "Why, I most certainly did not! What do you take me for?"

"All right, I'm sorry. I'm sure you wouldn't. But I know you never did believe Harry had any right to sit at his typewriter every weekend when there were so many more important jobs to do, as you would have put it. You thought he hadn't any excuse at all to call himself a writer."

Gramma looked sideways and down. "Well, p'raps so," she admitted. "But that was none of my affair. Anyway, I've thought of what I did with that box—out in the garage, that's where I put it, to get it out of the way with every closet in this house stuffed full."

And there it was, Gramma and Julia found when they opened up the dark little garage and started hunting, shoved way back in a corner.

"Of course!" said Gramma. "Of course!" And it seemed to Julia that she was tremendously relieved, as if she hadn't been too sure, after all, that the box would really be there. And when they brought it in, Mama discovered in no time that it must have been the story Daddy had been writing those last three days he was home that he had wanted her to find.

"This," she said, holding up what Julia knew was called a manuscript, "is what he meant me to pay attention to. This story is why he wanted Julia to be sure to tell me to go through his papers. I'm certain of it, because it's the only thing that's finished. But all the same, he didn't write it right off out of nothing. There are all sorts of notes he'd been making—it looks like for months."

"But, Celia, what on earth do you mean—talking as if he really gave Julia a message in her dream. I never heard of such nonsense in my life!"

"That may well be," and now Mama was shuffling through the pages and slipping them into order, "but whatever experience Julia was having, I'm going to pay attention to it. Harry's story will be a bit hard to follow—this is what you call a first draft, Julia—but tomorrow I'm going to begin typing out a copy of it that Uncle Hugh can read. I think I could manage

maybe an hour or so a day, and then more later on. Then we shall see what we shall see."

Julia and Greg and Gramma usually had dinner sitting at a card table next to Mama's bed so that they could all be together. But this evening she asked if they would mind her staying alone so that she could go on reading Daddy's story while she ate. She couldn't wait to see what he had done, and it wasn't easy making her way through his corrections and crossings-out and rewritings.

So it was while they were having dinner in the kitchen that Gramma told Greg all that had happened: about Julia and her dream and finding their father's story, with, of course, constant excited interruptions from Julia. Gramma asked Greg, just as if he were a grown-up, if he didn't agree with her that his mother was badly mistaken in her astonishing idea that his father had been sending a message through Julia about that story. "I can't get it into my head," she said, "that your mother would actually believe such a thing."

"Oh, I don't know, Gramma," said Greg, quite seriously, just as if he *was* a grown-up, thought Julia, but of course he had just turned nine in September. "I see something."

"What do you see?" asked Gramma suspiciously. Then, "You mean, you don't think it's a lot of nonsense?" she exclaimed, scandalized.

AVONDALE MIDDLE SCHOOL

"No, I don't. And I'll tell you why. When did Jule get knocked unconscious? The end of the war was November 11th, and Jule fell off the acting bar a little while before that. How could we find the exact date?"

Gramma pursed up her lips and put her head on one side as if she knew but wasn't telling. Greg stared around as though searching for some idea, and finally Gramma said grudgingly, "Well, you know where the bills are." She couldn't keep it back.

"You mean Dr. Silverman's!" Greg jumped up with Julia close behind him, ran into the living room where Mama's wicker desk was, got a box she kept the bills in, and came back to the table with it. In a moment or two he drew out Dr. Silverman's bill and looked it over, then up at them. "We don't need anybody to tell us when Dad's plane was shot down—October 31st. And Dr. Silverman met us at the hospital for Jule's X ray the very next morning, Sunday, November 1st."

Gramma and Julia stared at him, and nobody said a word. But the reason Julia was silent was because she didn't really understand. "But—but what—when was—?" she asked finally.

"Jule, November comes right after October. I *said,* 'the very next morning.' "

"Oh." And now they got up and went into the bedroom.

"Mom, we have proof. Dad's plane went down October 31st, and we met Dr. Silverman over at the hospital the next morning. So Jule was knocked out October 31st."

"Now I see," said Julia. And she really did. She saw herself getting up onto the hard table that was so uncomfortable, and the big heavy blanket being put over her that Greg said had lead in it to protect her from the rays—all but her head. And it had surprised her that the whole thing took only a second.

Mama held out her hand for the bill. "Greg, why didn't I think of it—the proof? The moment your father's plane was hit, he knew it was going down and that this was the end. And he thought of us. But the only one he could get through to was Julia, because she was all by herself in that state of unconsciousness, while you and I were busy about our worldly affairs. We weren't listening—we weren't open to him—he couldn't get through to us with his thought, but he could get to Julia." She stopped and seemed to reflect. "Yet who knows?" she went on. "Perhaps, after all, it was the special feeling between Julia and her father that made it possible for him to get through to her. Of course we can never know what actually happened, or why Julia had her dream—otherwise unexplainable when you think that afterwards she could pass on to me something she didn't understand herself."

"Well, I should think," said Gramma, "that in his last minutes he would be thinking about how much he cared for you and hoping that you would be able to get along all right without him. Not talking about going through some silly papers!" Gramma sounded dry and bitter and indignant.

"Mother, he'd already let me know what he felt about his family in every one of his letters he wrote home. Do you suppose there was ever the least doubt in my mind how he felt about us?"

13

Story

Before she began typing it, Mama read the story over three times to make certain she understood all of Daddy's crossings-out and rewritings. And as the days went by and she felt stronger, she began piling up the finished pages—"the fair copy," she told Julia it was called. But she would go back and look again at what Daddy had crossed out and rewritten in his very fine scrawl and not be satisfied with what she'd put, and do a page over. So it was quite a while before she got the story typed out in a way that satisfied her. Then she phoned Uncle Hugh and asked if he would like to read it.

He must have wanted to know what she thought of

it, because Julia heard her say, "Hugh, I think it's splendid. I can't believe how good it is. I think it's the best thing he's ever done, but perhaps, because he was my husband and I know so well how much he wanted to be a good writer, I'm not seeing it clear enough. So you must read it. When can you come over?"

Uncle Hugh came the following Saturday and had lunch with them. He had already heard, of course, about Mama's finding the story. But he hadn't been told about Julia's dream and how this tied up with the date on Dr. Silverman's bill and the time of Daddy's plane going down.

And when he was told—"It's extraordinary—absolutely extraordinary!" he said in a low voice.

"But you don't mean you *believe* it, Hugh!" demanded Gramma. "You don't mean you think the way Celia and Greg do—that the children's father was actually trying to get a message through to Celia about this piece of writing!"

Uncle Hugh's eyebrows went up. "Well, yes, Mother, somehow I do. I mean, I think there's a strong possibility."

"Oh!" she cried in disgust. "I never heard the like of it. Everybody in this house has gone foolish in the head. I'm discouraged with the lot of you—especially with Greg. Here I've always thought I could trust Greg, above everyone, to be a sensible human being. But even *he*—"

"Sorry, Grandma," said Greg, grinning at her. "I just believe in keeping an open mind."

"Open mind, my foot," cried Gramma, and got her black string bag and went off to the market as if this atmosphere of empty-headedness wasn't to be borne a minute longer.

While Julia and Greg did the dishes, Uncle Hugh sat on the couch in the living room and read Daddy's story. And Mama sat nearby with Patchy in her lap, stroking and stroking him, and watching Uncle Hugh's expression. She had some mending, but Julia, looking in now and then while she was drying a dish, noticed that Mama wasn't doing nearly as much mending as watching Uncle Hugh read. But she didn't say a single word.

Finally, when Uncle Hugh had finished, he looked up at the three of them. "Oh, yes," he said. "Yes, this should be published. It's very fine. It's as if, somehow—" and he stopped to think, "it's as if he knew at last exactly what he was about, exactly what he wanted to say in the way he wanted to say it."

"I know, Hugh, I know."

"Have you read your father's story, Greg?" asked Uncle Hugh.

Greg nodded. "I like it better than any other story he's written—that I've read. But I guess I don't understand it the way you two do."

Julia was watching Uncle Hugh. "Aren't you going to ask *me*? I read it—or I tried to, anyway."

"Julia, dear, I'm sorry. It never occurred to me that you would read it, because it isn't easy to understand."

"I know. And I didn't. I couldn't even read all of it —well, hardly any of it, because I got tired. But I like the name ever so much—'In the Hot Golden Berry Garden.' That's our berry garden, isn't it? And there's the part in Daddy's story about the little girl telling the story about the king and queen. Only it's different in his story—different from mine."

"Yours!" exclaimed Mama.

"How different, Julia? In what way do you mean?" asked Uncle Hugh.

Suddenly Julia had the oddest, quickest prick of knowing what she should say. "Oh, just different. Maybe I don't remember exactly—but different." In Daddy's story it was "the tall thin bossy queen and the little round kind king" instead of the way she'd had it, "the big fat bossy queen and the nice kind handsome king," which, she saw now, was just like Aunt Alex and Uncle Hugh. "Just think, if somebody takes Daddy's story, then I would see—I mean, it would turn out that my—"

"That your story will be published, too," said Mama. "Yes! And what I must do is send it to one magazine after another and never get discouraged if it keeps coming back."

But it did keep coming back, first from *The Delineator*, then from *McCall's*, then *The Woman's Home Com-*

panion, then *The Ladies' Home Journal,* and finally from *The Saturday Evening Post.* And Mama insisted on typing it all over again in between *The Woman's Home Companion* and *The Ladies' Home Journal* because it had begun to get shabby—dog-eared, Mama called it, which Julia thought was a funny, good word—and she refused to send it out that way. It had to be perfect.

One day in late spring when Uncle Hugh came over, he said to Mama, "Celia, you're still looking a very thin, pale girl—too pale. I think you're tired and need a vacation. How would you and Greg and Julia like to go up to Yosemite, come June, and camp by the river for a couple of weeks? I could get time off from the bank by then, and it seems to me you need a change."

"Oh, Mama—!" Julia was hopping up and down and clinging on to Uncle Hugh, so that his arm was pumped around. "Oh, *please?*" But Greg didn't say a word. He never did if he wanted something intensely, as if he didn't dare say anything or it wouldn't happen. But he must remember Yosemite too. Daddy had taken them up once when they were younger, and Julia remembered an endless meadow she'd run across as if she were flying, and tremendous gray cliffs with water tumbling over, and the river flowing, and their campfire in the dark, and being curled up in her sleeping bag, hearing the night sounds. "Please, please, please!"

"Julia, that will do now. Hugh, I would love it. But what about Alex? Wouldn't she—?"

"Mind, do you mean? *Alex?* I asked her if she'd like to come, knowing the answer ahead of time, and she looked at me and laughed. When had she ever wanted to go up in the mountains, she said, especially to camp? And what would she do with herself all day while we were off hiking? Anyhow, Celia, when shall we plan for?"

"I don't know. I'll have to ask at work and see what would fit in. If only some magazine would accept Harry's story, I could be a happy woman. Or in any case, happier than I have been."

Uncle Hugh was sitting with his elbows on his knees, and now he put his hands together in a peak the way he often did, Julia had noticed, when he was thinking. "I wonder—why not send it to *The Listener?* That's one of the best magazines in the country. I think the others haven't been right for it."

Mama looked at him in silence for a moment. "But *The Listener* doesn't seem right for it either. I don't know, Hugh—maybe there *is* no right one. I've about come to that conclusion."

"But you mean you're not going to send it *off* again?" demanded Julia. She couldn't believe it. What had been the use of "going through" her father's papers, then? And here came another small, strong thought tailing along behind. She'd never see her own story in print, after all. And she'd been looking forward to showing Maisie. She really had been sort of counting on it, to watch Maisie's face. And there wouldn't be one thing Maisie could say, like, "I'm glad *I'm* not a writer, and got my story printed." Of course she'd never say, "Golly, Julia!" but she'd be thinking it inside herself. She'd have to be.

"In a while, Julia—in a while I'll send it again," Mama was saying in answer to her question. "But the story really needs retyping."

"I could do it, Mom," said Greg. "Let me!"

"Oh, no, Greg. Thanks, dear, but I really want to. And I will, but not just right now. I guess you're right, Hugh, I'm tired. I need a rest."

Three weeks later, she and Greg and Julia got themselves packed up and went off to Yosemite with Uncle Hugh. Greg had a book about Egypt in case it rained too hard to go out, and Julia had a new book of fairy tales. But she couldn't imagine when she'd have time to read it.

As for Patchy, Bob couldn't feed him because he and his family were going away too. But Gramma said that of course she'd come over and feed him and see that he was all right. *Never,* Julia said to Mama, had she *ever* sounded like that about Patchy before.

14

Wonders and "Mrs. Woollards"

Julia had asked Uncle Hugh if Maisie could come along with them and he said, why, of course she could. But when Julia ran over, sizzling with excitement, and told Mrs. Woollard where Uncle Hugh was going to take them, and that they were going to camp for *two whole weeks,* and asked could Maisie come too, she frowned and shook her head.

"Oh, *Mama—!*" Maisie sounded absolutely finished, as if nothing good would ever happen to her again. And it was the first time Julia could remember Maisie letting on she wanted fiercely to do something Julia was going to do. "*Why* not—*why* not?"

"Because sooner or later, Maisie Woollard, Julia

would get you into trouble, *that's* why. Maybe it's not always entirely your fault, Julia," Mrs. Woollard said, "but somehow it happens—trouble. The two of you would go off the trail and get lost, or you'd climb a tree and fall, or go into a cave, or—Lord knows, I can't imagine what you'd think up to do. You're beyond me, Julia, and I'm not sitting here in this house for two solid weeks wondering what in heaven's name you're getting Maisie into. That I'm not. I couldn't face it."

"But I wouldn't *go* off the trail, Mama, or into any cave, or climb a tree, I promise you I wouldn't. And I've never *been* camping. It's not fair—it's not fair—!"

"No, it's no use, Maisie, I'm not having it. The whole thing would happen before you'd even know what you were up to. Julia never *means* to do anything —it just doesn't turn out right. But I'll tell you what, Maisie," and Mrs. Woollard put her hand out and rather awkwardly stroked Maisie's hair, "we'll go along, you and me, and spend the week with Aunt Nellie. How would you like that?"

"I wouldn't like it one bit!" shouted Maisie (Julia had never, never heard her shout at her mother), "I don't *want* to go along to Aunt Nellie's and spend a week. I'd hate it! What fun would that be?" And she turned away and ran stamping and sobbing upstairs.

The three of them had been standing in the front hall all this time, and Julia could hear Maisie in her room carrying on something fearful. Now she noticed those two red spots in Mrs. Woollard's cheeks she'd seen before, and all at once she didn't know where to look. "Well, I'm sorry, Mrs. Woollard," she said in a faint voice, and got herself out, and went home.

But you never can tell about people. Saturday morning, round about seven o'clock, just after Uncle Hugh had parked his car and come in to get their bags, here was Maisie at the front door.

"What d'you s'pose, Julia! You'll never guess! We're going to my Aunt Nellie's tomorrow, Mama and me, and it's near the ocean and I'm going to be down on the beach and go in swimming *every single day* — what d'you think about *that*? Aren't I the luckiest thing? I'm the luckiest thing in the world! I'd a *million* times rather go to the beach than up into the boring old mountains—lucky, lucky, lucky me," sang Maisie, running down the front steps before Julia could answer a single word, and on across the street. "Lucky, lucky, lucky, lucky—!" and up her front walk, and up the steps, and slammed the door behind her.

Well, it was just as Mrs. Woollard had known it would be about Julia. First afternoon, right off—a "Mrs. Woollard thing," as Julia always called them afterwards.

It was only two hundred miles from Berkeley to

Yosemite, so there was plenty of time to get their camp by the side of the Merced River in order before dinner. Soon they had everything unpacked, and Uncle Hugh and Greg got the two tents up, one for them and the other for Julia and Mama.

Uncle Hugh had brought something that Julia didn't remember the Redferns having when they'd been here before. It was a cupboard to hold their food, with a ring on the top so that he could hitch a rope through it. When he'd thrown the other end of the rope over a high limb above their camp and drawn the cupboard up out of arm's reach, he tied that end firmly to a small lower limb. This way, he could draw the cupboard up and down as it was needed.

"But why up so high, Uncle Hugh?"

"Bears, Julia," he said. "We wouldn't have a bite to eat but our pancake flour if those bears got at it. And don't think they couldn't get that cupboard open. I honestly think, if there's food to be had, and it's within paw reach, they can get anything. Oh, and by the way, Julia. Remember always to let the animals mind their business while we mind ours. Now remember that."

When all was in order, they set off across the big central meadow Julia remembered, headed for the majestic double Yosemite falls—upper and lower—plunging down over the cliff in thick spurts and gouts of water, right up there ahead of them. And the sound of the water thundering against rock filled the air, together with the hurrying and smashing of the river over its boulders and the rush of the wind in the treetops.

They had to go through a woods before they got to the foot of the lower falls, and it was here that the first Mrs. Woollard thing happened. Mama and Uncle Hugh and Greg were going on ahead, Uncle Hugh and Greg singing "Quiet Sandy."

> My name is Quiet Sandy
> And I like to be my lone—
> I love the bounding, bouncing waves,
> The ocean is my home.
>
> For I'm a bounding bounder
> As I'm bounding over the sea—
> O-o-oh, up in the North
> In the Firth of Forth,
> That is the pla-a-ace for me!

And then they were laughing and talking and not paying any attention to Julia because Mama and Uncle Hugh were a little way ahead with Greg right behind, so Mama probably thought Julia was with Greg. But she wasn't. She was quite a bit behind, and she'd seen bears.

There they were—a whole group of them, around a garbage can some way over to the right. Her first real, honest-to-goodness bears! She had an apple she'd taken a bite or two out of, and now she held it out

temptingly and moved toward them. And they stood there watching her, three or four of them on their hind legs like stout, dignified gentlemen with large stomachs, wearing heavy brown fur coats. She had almost reached them when two of them dropped on all fours.

"Here, bears," she called, as she would have called Patchy. "A nice apple. Here, bears—here, bears—"

The two were shambling toward her, when there was an exclamation from Mama, who must have heard Julia calling in that high, fetching voice. And in a breath or two, or so it seemed, she'd reached Julia and was yanking her away. Uncle Hugh said afterwards he hadn't heard anything, but suddenly Mama wasn't there, and when he turned, he'd never seen a woman cover ground so fast.

"Julia, *never* do that again—*never, never,* do you hear me?" she was saying in a fierce, breathless voice right into Julia's face. "We *told* you to keep away from the wild animals. We told you so carefully. Weren't you paying attention?" Julia couldn't answer. "If a bear got that apple," Mama went on, "he'd want more. And if you didn't have more, who knows *what* he'd do!"

"I know what he'd do," said Greg pleasantly. "When the lucky bear had golloped up that apple, he'd have just kept right on going, right up your arm, Jule."

Julia shuddered. Sharp, painful prickles ran over her from head to foot.

"Don't you remember, Julia," said Uncle Hugh almost sternly (and when had he *ever* been stern with her?), "that we said that you must always leave the animals to go about their business while we go about ours?"

"Yes," she said in a faint, shamed voice, "now I do." But, oh, when she'd actually seen the bears, it had all gone right out of her head, she'd so wanted them to come close and to have her apple.

"Not bright," said Greg. "That's Jule's trouble— not bright," and he turned and continued his happy way toward the falls. Julia, holding Uncle Hugh's hand on one side and Mama's on the other, went along thinking about bears, and particularly a bear after he'd finished the apple, if she'd managed to give it to him.

But as soon as they came out of the woods and arrived at the bridge that crossed the torrent booming away from the foot of the falls, she forgot about bears. She gasped, looking up. She couldn't believe it. She'd never seen anything like it that she could remember— this welter of white, visible thunder. And you couldn't go onto the bridge without getting soaking wet from the spray.

"Just think!" shouted Uncle Hugh. "And here it is June, when the falls are supposed to be down to a thread."

They couldn't possibly cross over, though some people were, with raincoats on and with shawls over their heads. "Why didn't *we* bring raincoats?" shouted Julia, but nobody heard her. And they stood there and gazed and gaped until they'd had their fill, though Julia hadn't. She could have gone on and on looking and listening. It satisfied her soul: this thunder, this gigantic plunge of water, as if it weighed tons and tons. And then the fury of upheaval at the bottom.

And so Julia had seen one Wonder and had one Mrs. Woollard thing happen. Now, this very night, she saw another Wonder. After dinner, when it was dark, she noticed everybody wandering along the trail past their camp, all in the same direction. There had been glimmers of campfires among the trees and delectable smells wafting around of dinners cooking. Then there were the clinks of dishes and cutlery and pans being washed and put away, and now there were the people going past.

"Where are they all headed, Uncle Hugh?"

"For the same place we're going—"

"But what *for*—what *for?*"

"Surprise," said Greg. "You wait and see."

The place was the Center at Camp Curry, and there they all stood in the darkness, patiently waiting, patiently looking up, Julia noticed. Up at Glacier Point, Uncle Hugh said, though you couldn't see a thing— the whole valley was pitch black.

"D'you remember being up there last time we were here, Julia, up at Glacier Point?" asked Mama.

"I do," said Greg. "I remember exactly."

"It's so high up there," said Mama, "it takes your breath away to look over. You were scared, Julia. Your eyes were enormous, and yet we couldn't get you to leave. You clung to the guardrail and went right on looking down over the edge—everything all laid out so tiny down here, the buildings and river and roads and trees. You couldn't seem to have enough of looking."

Oh, thought Julia, yes. She was beginning to get it back. And she remembered the birds, how they'd lift their wings and flutter, or simply float out into the tremendous deeps of the air. While if *she* had slipped under the guardrail and stepped too close to the edge —but, no—*no!*

"How many feet down to the valley here is it from Glacier Point, Uncle Hugh?" asked Greg.

"Almost a mile. I don't remember just how many feet, but almost a mile."

"And now the fi—"

"Sh-sh!" said Mama quickly.

"Oh, *what?*" begged Julia. But nobody would tell, and so she watched too, her head way back, and presently flames sprang up against the black sky all strewn with stars, billions and billions more stars than she'd ever seen in the city and all blazing away like Billy-ho. Then the flames up at Glacier Point leaped higher and higher until Julia knew what they had up there was a gigantic bonfire. What a fine idea—but when she said this to Greg, he just laughed.

"You think everybody's here to see an old bonfire? All these people? You just wait!"

And presently Julia's eyes widened in the dark, because there began to be a rain of fire from Glacier Point, and it kept pouring and pouring down like a waterfall turned to flame. For the men up there were constantly feeding that great mass of burning logs and pushing forward the embers over the edge, so that they kept the shape of a broad flaming fall almost the entire length of the drop.

Then, as if the firefall weren't enough, a lady began singing "By the Waters of Minnetonka," just loud enough for you to hear but not too loud, and when that was finished, "The Indian Love Call." "My, my," said Mama. "Different from last time. What was it then?" And when the last few embers had been pushed over, Julia drew a big, trembling breath and hadn't a word to say for herself all the way back to camp.

"Didn't you like it, Julia?" asked Mama.

"Oh, yes. Yes, I *did.*" Then, after a bit, "But just think, I won't ever see it again."

"I don't know why not—unless you're asleep. They have it every night. But I think I'll go only once in a while, so that it won't become ordinary."

"But how could it—ever? And why don't I remember it? And the falls over by the bridge?"

"Because last time you were asleep before eight o'clock every night after walking all day, and you don't remember the falls because they were all dried up."

The next Wonder happened toward the end of the last week, when they were coming back from Bridalveil Fall along the length of the valley facing Half Dome. "Ploughed out by ice, by glaciers," Uncle Hugh was telling them about the valley. "Cut and ground and sheered and scoured out over thousands and thousands of years—no, millions." Yes, that huge dome there at the other end of the valley might have been chopped through with a single stroke, leaving half of it standing.

The sun had set by now, perhaps twenty minutes before, and the sky was beginning to take on the powerful gemlike blue of early dusk, when all at once Julia saw the sky light up again all salmon pink and the gray rock of Half Dome turn a rich, deep apricot.

"But why—why?" exclaimed Julia. "I thought the sun had already set. Is it coming back? Is it going to be morning again already?"

"Oh, Jule!" said Greg. "As if it could be morning now. I think this is called—" but he couldn't get back what it was called.

"Afterglow," said Uncle Hugh. "I've just thought of it. It's the reflection of the sun's rays on particles of dust high in the atmosphere—or maybe this reflection is coming from the snowfields."

They stood and watched while the radiance gradually faded, then they wandered back to camp. And Uncle Hugh told them about the tremendous eruption of a volcano called Krakatoa which had turned the sunsets of the world deep red for years afterwards because of the fine volcanic dust that had wound around the earth and stayed there.

Then came a Mrs. Woollard thing on the next to the last day of their stay in Yosemite. They had been going single file along a trail with a sharp drop to the left, Greg going on ahead, with Julia in the middle, and then Mama and Uncle Hugh. Now they came to a small meadow with a roosting of those giant boulders up at the back. Uncle Hugh proposed that they stop for a little and rest and enjoy the view out beyond the trail from the meadow. Greg went to climb on the boulders, and of course Julia followed him.

"Julia," said Mama, "you are not to go on the boulders. They're too big and you might fall in between."

So Julia played on the ground nearby, watching Greg and calling out to him and, now and then, to Mama and Uncle Hugh, and they would turn every few minutes to see that she was still there, and to watch that she got into no mischief.

But suddenly, there in the grass, Julia saw a most beautiful snake. He was a brown snake with white rings. He looked smooth and glossy as enamel and Julia wanted more than anything she could think of to touch him, to hold him, to *feel* his smooth, slim, lithe glossiness, and to stroke his head.

"I won't hurt you," she whispered, and watched him while he watched her out of his bright unblinking eyes with his head turned toward her and his thready tongue flickering in and out. But now he seemed to have had enough of her and glided away through the grass. Julia followed him as he made his way onto the higher ground behind the boulders, over the hillock, and down to the trail on the other side where it continued on past the rocks. She was just in time to see him ripple across the trail, over the edge, and down the slope. And Julia, refusing to give him up, went after him.

She squatted down, then went head first on her stomach, slowly at the beginning, one hand out to catch hold of his tail. But he disappeared, and Julia kept going, sliding down the steep slope ever more rapidly, until she came to a halt on a ledge just wide enough to hold her. Now it came over her in a wave of hot terror—what would Mama say? "If I'm killed, she'll never forgive me—" She looked up, but Greg was in among the rocks and she was too bitterly ashamed to call out to him or to Mama and Uncle Hugh. Mrs. Woollard! she thought. Julia could just hear her.

Carefully, carefully, she twisted herself around to face uphill, then reached out a hand to grasp a little tough-looking bush so that she could draw herself up a foot or two. And reached out for another, then another, and another, always drawing herself up very slowly and carefully. She had a feeling she couldn't

have explained that if she tried to force herself up fast, all the little rocks beneath her would begin sliding out from under her and she would go with them. Also, if she yanked at the little bushes, they might come out by the roots.

"Oh, Mama—Mama," she whispered, her voice shaking, and she began to cry a little—just a little, because she needed all her strength. And when she saw the top of the slope drawing near, she took heart and pulled herself up more strongly until at last she lay, stomach down, across the trail. She wiped her dusty hands across her tears and was just commencing to steal around the rocks to find out if she'd been missed, when here came Mama and Uncle Hugh.

"Julia! Where in the name of heaven have you been?" cried Mama. "When I turned and couldn't see you and you didn't answer me—"

"I'm all right."

"No, you are *not* all right. You look all roughed up and dusty and as if you've been crying. What happened?"

"I'm all right, Mama. I *am,* I tell you. What *could* have happened?"

Julia Redfern, what a fib of a question. And she would say no more, and Mama never did find out about the beautiful snake, which Julia discovered later was a king snake and not poisonous.

Well, so there! she thought.

The last Wonder happened on the very last evening. Mama was in the tent getting ready for bed and brushing out her long hair, and Uncle Hugh was in his, and Julia and Greg were standing out by the campfire. They'd all been sitting around it, talking, after coming back from the firefall, and now the campfire had faded to a few coals. Julia looked up at the sky at all those blazing points of light, hoping she would be able to tell Maisie just how the firefall was, and how these mountain stars seemed a sea of stars. And all at once one of them, one of the biggest and most brilliant, swooped right down across the sky.

Julia's breath stopped. Why, it had actually happened! She had *seen* a falling star. She'd *seen* it. She had heard people talk about falling stars, but she had never believed there were such things—after all, how could a star fall? And she turned to tell Greg and to ask him about this, but he had gone.

Slowly she went into Mama's and her tent, and Mama was in bed. She got undressed and into her sleeping bag on the camp cot and curled up.

"Mama?"

"Yes, dear?"

"Could the sun fall?" She pictured it—a dreadful sight, their sun whizzing down across the sky and then everything all dark and cold forever after. Or would it be? But surely, if there were no more sun—

"Of course not," said Mama in a sleepy voice.

"Then how about the moon? Couldn't the moon fall if a star could?"

"I don't know, Julia. Oh, of course not. The moon couldn't possibly fall."

"But why *not*? If a star falls."

"But it isn't a star falling. A star is a far-off sun. And what we call falling stars are meteors, chunks of metal getting red hot when they come shooting into our atmosphere. Greg and I talked about this once."

"What's atmosphere?"

"Oh, Julia, Julia dear—that will do. I was so ready to go to sleep." Silence. And then presently Mama said, as if she'd been thinking, "Atmosphere is the dust and gases around our earth. And the moon goes round the earth, and the earth goes round the sun, and they all go round and round and none of them can fall. So now go to sleep."

> The moon goes round the earth
> And the earth goes round the sun.
> And they all go round and round
>   and round
> And none of them *can* fall down.

sang Julia to herself, silently, inside her head.

> The earth goes round the moon.
> And the sun goes round the—

And she was asleep.

15

Theron W. Makepeace

When they got home at about seven thirty the next evening, everyone hungry for dinner, there was a collection of mail on the living room table. Gramma, when she came over to feed Patchy, had left it after gathering it up every day from under the letter slot in the front door.

Mama slid the letters and bills and folders aside one by one to see what was there. But she left a big brown envelope without opening it while she slit the tops of the three letters.

"Why, Celia," said Uncle Hugh, who had just come in with her suitcase, "it's from *The Listener*. Why don't you open it?"

"Because I know what it'll say and it's too depressing." Mama hadn't put on weight up at Yosemite because, though they'd all eaten more than they did at home, they'd walked almost all day every day. But she was brown and looked much better than she had in months. Yet now, Julia saw, she had her old sad expression back again.

"But I thought," said Greg, "that you weren't going to type Dad's story over again and send it off before we left."

"I didn't type it over, Greg. But I did send it off about three weeks before we left. Well, right after Uncle Hugh was here, talking about going up to the mountains, as a matter of fact. I thought that if *The Listener* really wanted it, they wouldn't mind a bent page or two. Don't bother with it."

"But if you don't mind, Celia, I will bother with it," said Uncle Hugh. "May I?"

"If you like."

And so Uncle Hugh did, and read over the letter that was attached to Daddy's manuscript. "I see you sent the story as if Harry had sent it—used his name to sign your letter to them. Listen to this in reply.

Dear Mr. Redfern:
   We are very pleased to have your story, "In the Hot Golden Berry Garden," and would like to publish it if you could clear up some confusing points, marked in the margins.
   On the whole, the story is beautifully worked

out, and it is just those five places that we think could be improved upon.

If you agree with us, we will pay $300 upon publication.

We all feel that this story seems to be a chapter in a novel. If you have a novel in mind, we would be very interested to see the finished manuscript. As you know, we are part of the publishing house Thurlow, Biggs, and Adams.

We look forward to hearing from you.

Sincerely yours,

Theron W. Makepeace

Theron W. Makepeace
Editor
The Listener

Mama stared at Uncle Hugh. "Why, I can't believe it, Hugh, even though I knew it should be published! It's happened—at last it's happened! Oh, if only—"

"If only what, Mama? If only *what?*" asked Julia intensely.

"If only your father could know that someone thinks as I do—that he really was a writer—"

"And you *will* try to clear up those places they've marked in the margins?" Uncle Hugh was leafing through the manuscript and had stopped and was reading over a page. "Ye-es," he said, "I remember this part, that it puzzled me, too."

"No," said Mama. "I can't."

Greg and Julia and Uncle Hugh looked at her in shocked amazement. "What do you mean, you can't?" he asked.

"I mean, I wouldn't. I'm not a writer, and I wouldn't lay a finger on Harry's story. It's his, and he would hate to have anyone fiddling around with it, including me. He was so particular about every word, and I don't even know if he'd agree that those places should be changed. Don't you see, Hugh? Would *you* want someone rewriting parts of your story? Even if they were only sentences here and there? Would you let anyone write in so much as a word? You'd hate it. You know you would!"

Uncle Hugh frowned and thought this over. Then he picked up the story and began going over it again.

"But, Mom," said Greg, sounding troubled and sharply disappointed, "not even to get Dad's story published?"

"No, Greg, not even to get his story published. I don't think he'd want it that way."

"Well, *I* do," burst out Julia. "*I* do—and I think it's mean and awful keeping his story in the dark. I don't think he'd want it kept in the dark after all the work he went to, writing it. And he *told* me you were to go through his papers. So why would he tell me that if it's all no use and you're not going to let anything happen?" She'd been looking up at Mama with blazing, indignant eyes and a hot face. She couldn't understand

Mama at all after Mr. What's-his-name wanting Daddy's story so much, when all the others had turned it down.

"Why, Julia—" said Mama, thoroughly astonished, and she didn't, somehow, sound nearly so certain now. Actually, she looked shaken.

"Celia," said Uncle Hugh, "I think Julia's right. And do you know, it isn't a matter of rewriting a great deal. It's a matter of changing a word or two here and there, except for this place, here, where two sentences, as I see it, would have to be rewritten. I think you must reconsider. I'm like Julia, I think it would be very unfair to keep Harry's story out of the magazine because of a few slight changes that could be made."

There was silence while they all studied Mama, who didn't say anything for a moment. Then, "Give me the story, Hugh. Let me see." And after a little, "Oh, I don't know—perhaps you're right. And here I was so sure of myself!"

All at once Julia slipped away and left Mama and Uncle Hugh and Greg talking in the living room. Out in the kitchen she rang Gramma's phone number and when she answered, "Hello, Gram, we're home."

"Yes, I had an idea you were, because I saw Patchy taking off down the street a few minutes ago as if he knew exactly where he was going."

"Gramma, you'll never guess. We have a letter from someone who wants to print Daddy's story in the very *best* magazine, and he wants to know if Daddy was going to write a novel and could he see it when it's finished. What do you think of *that*?" demanded Julia in stern triumph. "He really was a writer, and now you can't say he wasn't."

There was quite a silence at the other end of the wire. Then, "Well, I'll be jiggered," said Gramma in a low voice at last.

Now here came Mama. "Is that Gramma?" and she took the receiver. "Has Julia told you, Mother?"

Brief answer at the other end. Probably just yes, thought Julia.

"Well, what do you think?" asked Mama. "You never did believe in Harry, did you? Won't you finally have to admit that there *was* something to the idea that he was a writer?"

Another brief answer. And then a bit more.

"Well, I'm glad," said Mama. "I'm very glad to hear that."

Now a question.

"Three hundred dollars," answered Mama. "Imagine that! And all because of Julia. It still seems to me her dream wasn't just some passing, meaningless train of fancies. At least I can't believe it was."

Reply from Gramma.

"All right," said Mama, "have it your way. But another thing—Julia got indignant with me because I was refusing to make a few little changes. She said something about my keeping her father's story 'in the dark' if I didn't make them, and somehow I've had to change my mind. What do you think of that?''

A remark or two and then another question, to which Mama replied that she was feeling herself again, after all these months, and that they'd had a fine and happy time. "We'll see you tomorrow, then, Mother —and we'll be watching for Patchy. Goodbye, dear.''

Mama hung up and turned and put her arms around Julia. "You heard what I said to Gramma—that it wasn't just some sort of trick of the mind or coincidence that you got Daddy's message to give to us. But Gramma can't see it that way. What a most mysterious thing it all is, Julia. And to think that it happened to us.''

Mysterious. Most mys-teri-ous, said Julia to herself. Oh, yes, that was her best word yet, and she would use it—probably quite often.

"Now," said Mama, getting up, "go out and call Patchy and I'll start dinner. Uncle Hugh's going to stay and eat with us before going home.''

So Julia ran into the other room, where Greg was reading his father's story all over again, and gave Uncle Hugh a sudden, excited hug, then went outside. "Mys-teeeri-ous,'' she said aloud to herself, savoring it. "Most, *most* mys-teeeri-ous!''

She looked across at Maisie's house and it was all dark with just one little dim light in the upstairs front bedroom. So then maybe Maisie and her mother still weren't home from Aunt Nellie's and poor Mr. Woollard had had to eat all by himself again, a fried egg on a piece of burned toast, and an old leftover slice of dry cake and three or four cups of coffee. And now there he was, upstairs in bed already with his newspaper and nothing else to do.

Julia went out into the garden and along the path between the berry bushes to the little open place where a long time ago she had first told her story about the big fat bossy queen and the nice kind handsome king to the Japanese dolls and Sister and Patchy-cat, and Daddy had sung "Where Do Flies Go?" She stood there, looking and listening.

> Tell me, tell me,
> Where do flies go *(sang Julia, quietly)*
> In - the - win-ter - time?
> Do they go to gay Par-eeee?
> Or do they fly
> Like swallows in the sky
> To some distant foreign clime?
> Tell me, tell me,
> Where do flies go
> In - the - win-ter - time?

That used to be her favorite song of his. And to think that she'd wondered and wondered what a "four and climb" could be until she'd asked him what it meant and he'd explained to her that it was a "foreign clime," a distant place, a far-off climate. What a funny little kid.

"Patchy!" she called. "Patchy-cat, we're home—!" No Patchy.

Now the moon had moved up behind the leaves of the buckeye and was sending down sprinkles of moonlight onto the open place and Julia. A few early crickets were beginning to try a scrape or two, and she could smell pine and eucalyptus and rose geranium. Yes, everything was just the same.

But—*no,* she thought. Where was the grinling?

"Grinling? Hullo, grinling—" Nothing happened. She wasn't the least scared. She didn't feel a bit like running inside with her heart thumping. So then what had happened—had he changed? Was he a good, friendly grinling now, instead of a mean, scarey one? She'd never have believed it. To think that she had once been too afraid to come out here alone in the dark, afraid with a queer, thrilling, tense sort of afraidness—but now, no longer. She couldn't understand it. And then, how still more strange. Because she was a little disappointed. Maybe the poor old grinling had gotten discouraged and gone away because he knew it was no use staying around. Maybe he'd gone over to Maisie's.

Julia chuckled and went back along the path between the berry vines and out onto the sidewalk.

"Patchy—" she called, running toward Gramma's, "Patchy-cat—" and there, far off down the block, she saw a small scudding shape under the streetlamp, a dark shape with a white patch on its back, a white ear, and a white tip to its tail. *"Patchy—Patchy—Patchy!"*

He came at a gallop, and she caught him up and buried her face in his cool, clean, night-smelling fur, then turned and trotted along for home, holding him and talking to him and asking him how on earth he'd known they were here and that it was time for him to come. And when they drew near the house, he struggled to get down, probably, she thought, because she wasn't going fast enough. He dashed on ahead, in along the walk, and onto the porch with his tail straight up and quivering. And when she continued at a trot, he suddenly got up on his hind legs and with one front paw gave the knob on the screen door a couple of impatient bats as if to say, "Well, come on, you old slow poke, you! I'm *starved—*"

"So am I, Patchy, so am I!" And she ran up the steps.

———◆———

(Continued in *Julia and the Hand of God*)